PRAISE FOR
THE COOKING CLASS MYSTERIES

Dying for Dinner

"Love it! *Dying for Dinner* stands out from the crowded culinary mystery genre . . . Laced with delicious recipes [that] complement the book perfectly."

—*Roundtable Reviews*

"Annie and Eve make a great duo . . . Should appeal to a wide variety of readers." —*CA Reviews*

Dead Men Don't Get the Munchies

"Another highly entertaining culinary mystery . . . Miranda Bliss does an exceptional job creating a light, whimsical read." —*Roundtable Reviews*

"I would recommend this book to anyone who likes fun, adventure, and a bit of the unexplained." —*MyShelf.com*

"Bliss entices readers with captivating characters and a fun, scintillating mystery. A host of mouth-watering recipes is the perfect addition to the zany adventures of protagonist Annie." —*Romantic Times*

"Lighthearted fun." —*Cozy Library*

Murder on the Menu

"A nice blend of culinary mystery and romance. *Murder on the Menu* winds up nicely with a surprising twist and a number of scrumptious recipes."   —*Roundtable Reviews*

"A fun, entertaining mystery . . . Recommended reading— but be sure to eat first!"   —*The Romance Readers Connection*

Cooking Up Murder

"Charming . . . A blissful whodunit that is filled with some very funny scenes and characters who care about each other."   —*Midwest Book Review*

"The writing is spellbinding. The blend of mystery, humor, and romance keeps the reader hooked to the pages. The characters are entertaining, and it is not surprising that I find myself eager to read more about this duo. The addition of recipes in the back of the book only adds to its charm. Culinary-mystery fans will need to add this book to their reading piles."   —*Roundtable Reviews*

"A fun, quick read. A new twist on the favorite culinary mysteries."   —*The Mystery Reader*

"Light and breezy, touched with humor and a bit of romance. The protagonists are spunky and adventurous, and readers will be cheering for this delectable duo to crack the case."   —*Romantic Times*

continued . . .

Berkley Prime Crime titles by Miranda Bliss

COOKING UP MURDER
MURDER ON THE MENU
DEAD MEN DON'T GET THE MUNCHIES
DYING FOR DINNER
MURDER HAS A SWEET TOOTH

Murder Has a Sweet Tooth

MIRANDA BLISS

BERKLEY PRIME CRIME, NEW YORK

THE BERKLEY PUBLISHING GROUP
Published by the Penguin Group
Penguin Group (USA) Inc.
375 Hudson Street, New York, New York 10014, USA
Penguin Group (Canada), 90 Eglinton Avenue East, Suite 700, Toronto, Ontario M4P 2Y3, Canada
(a division of Pearson Penguin Canada Inc.)
Penguin Books Ltd., 80 Strand, London WC2R 0RL, England
Penguin Group Ireland, 25 St. Stephen's Green, Dublin 2, Ireland (a division of Penguin Books Ltd.)
Penguin Group (Australia), 250 Camberwell Road, Camberwell, Victoria 3124, Australia
(a division of Pearson Australia Group Pty. Ltd.)
Penguin Books India Pvt. Ltd., 11 Community Centre, Panchsheel Park, New Delhi—110 017, India
Penguin Group (NZ), 67 Apollo Drive, Rosedale, North Shore 0632, New Zealand
(a division of Pearson New Zealand Ltd.)
Penguin Books (South Africa) (Pty.) Ltd., 24 Sturdee Avenue, Rosebank, Johannesburg 2196,
South Africa

Penguin Books Ltd., Registered Offices: 80 Strand, London WC2R 0RL, England

This is a work of fiction. Names, characters, places, and incidents either are the product of the author's imagination or are used fictitiously, and any resemblance to actual persons, living or dead, business establishments, events, or locales is entirely coincidental. The publisher does not have any control over and does not assume any responsibility for author or third-party websites or their content.

PUBLISHER'S NOTE: The recipes contained in this book are to be followed exactly as written. The publisher is not responsible for your specific health or allergy needs that may require medical supervision. The publisher is not responsible for any adverse reactions to the recipes contained in this book.

MURDER HAS A SWEET TOOTH

A Berkley Prime Crime Book / published by arrangement with the author

PRINTING HISTORY
Berkley Prime Crime mass-market edition / December 2009

Copyright © 2009 by Penguin Group (USA) Inc.
Cover illustration by Stephanie Power.
Cover design by Rita Frangie.
Interior text design by Kristin del Rosario.

All rights reserved.
No part of this book may be reproduced, scanned, or distributed in any printed or electronic form without permission. Please do not participate in or encourage piracy of copyrighted materials in violation of the author's rights. Purchase only authorized editions.
For information, address: The Berkley Publishing Group,
a division of Penguin Group (USA) Inc.,
375 Hudson Street, New York, New York 10014.

ISBN: 978-0-425-23160-9

BERKLEY® PRIME CRIME
Berkley Prime Crime Books are published by The Berkley Publishing Group,
a division of Penguin Group (USA) Inc.,
375 Hudson Street, New York, New York 10014.
BERKLEY® PRIME CRIME and the PRIME CRIME logo are trademarks of Penguin Group (USA) Inc.

PRINTED IN THE UNITED STATES OF AMERICA

10   9   8   7   6   5   4   3   2   1

If you purchased this book without a cover, you should be aware that this book is stolen property. It was reported as "unsold and destroyed" to the publisher, and neither the author nor the publisher has received any payment for this "stripped book."

For all the friends and relatives
who've helped Annie and Eve in their
own way by contributing recipes to the
Cooking Class Mysteries

One

Larry turned around, his wallet heavy, and he glanced up at the shade of brown as usual... as accurate. He's consistent. He gave a careful thumbnail and... random... about his work.

...

One

✖

BELIEVE IT OR NOT, THERE ARE ACTUALLY SOME people who think I'm a jim-dandy detective.

Even after solving four cases, it blows me out of the water just to think about it.

I mean, I don't look like a detective. I'm short and curvy, a former bank teller whose hair is too curly and a shade of brown as ordinary as acorns. I'm a conservative dresser, a careful thinker, and as cautious about investigating murders as I am when it comes to everything from deciding what to order for Saturday night takeout to choosing the flowers for my upcoming wedding. I love clothes—as long as they're as matter-of-fact as I am. I love shoes—provided the heels aren't too high and the toes aren't too pointy. I love color, all color—as long as it comes in shades of beige.

And private detectives are supposed to be daring and flashy, right?

But talk to my best friend, Eve, and she'll tell you that there's a lot more to me than meets the eye. Eve's investigated a few cases with me and though she's been there at my side through thick and thin, she doesn't always get it, not when it comes to clues and suspects. She doesn't understand that for me, solving a murder is like putting together a puzzle. Since I'm all about neatness, all about order, and I refuse to move forward until I find every one of those flat-sided pieces that make it possible to build the frame and from there, to fit all the funny-shaped pieces inside, I don't stop until I have all the answers. I'm logical and I'm methodical, and I don't like when things are out of place.

And private detectives are supposed to be freewheeling free thinkers, right?

Then there's Jim MacDonald, the love of my life and the hottest hunk to come out of Scotland since Mel Gibson wore a kilt. Jim may not always be happy when I get involved with a murder investigation, but he's always supportive. He's as impressed by my detective skills as I am baffled that he (or anyone, for that matter) loves to cook. When it comes to trying to work out the details of a crime, he's a great brainstormer, and more times than I like to remember, he's put himself in harm's way to save my neck. Yeah, I'm nuts about him.

And private detectives are supposed to be loners, right?

Even Tyler Cooper, Arlington, Virginia, homicide detective, has had to admit (well, a time or two, anyway) that I'm smarter than the average PI and I get better results. In his own hard-nosed, hardheaded way, Tyler lets me know that he values my help. For one thing, now that he and Eve are dating again (they were once engaged and when it ended, it wasn't pretty), Tyler's treating Eve like a queen. Just like she deserves. For another, he's actually admitted that sometimes, an amateur can gain access to places and people that a professional can't. He shows his appreciation by dropping hints about where I should go to investigate and who I should talk to.

And private detectives aren't supposed to get along with the police, right?

I've even heard our friend Norman Applebaum sing my praises as a detective and, believe me, I didn't think that would ever happen, not after I found out in the course of an investigation that he wasn't who we all thought he was, and that he'd once been in prison. Of course, since then, Norman realized that he could turn the missteps of his youth into a whole new career. In addition to running his gourmet cooking store, Très Bonne Cuisine, Norman now hosts *The Cooking Con*, a wildly popular cable TV show. In fact, since I'm all about details, I've just proofread the final manuscript of Norman's new cookbook, *Prison Potluck*. It is destined to be a bestseller, and I am thrilled for him.

And private detectives (well, at least the ones on TV) are often disgruntled malcontents, right?

It's all so crazy, sometimes I have to tell myself I'm not dreaming. I mean, me, Annie Capshaw, once divorced and now engaged and the business manager of Jim's wonderful restaurant . . . me, a detective? But then, maybe that's why I find solutions to cases when even Tyler can't: I'm not the kind of detective anyone expects. It certainly helps encourage me when I think how much my friends admire what I do. They provide a boost, and, sometimes, backup. They believe in me, even when I don't always believe in myself.

That afternoon as I stood on Jim's front porch, I wondered what they'd say if they knew that my detective skills had failed me completely.

The thought sat in my stomach like the remains of the BLT I'd tried to make for lunch that afternoon. I'd burned some of the bacon to a crisp. Some of it, I hadn't cooked enough; it was floppy and greasy. When I tried to slice the sandwich into perfect pieces the way Jim always does, the tomato squished.

I pushed off from the window where I had my nose pressed against the glass and grumbled. Just like my stomach did.

In fact, I was so busy feeling inadequate and incapable of looking into even this, what should have been the simplest and the easiest-to-investigate mystery, I didn't hear Jim's car pull into the driveway.

Which explains why I jumped a mile when I heard him behind me.

"You're not trying to do something you shouldn't be doing, are ye, Annie?"

I pressed a hand to the front of my navy spring-weight jacket, the better to keep my heart from bursting through my ribs. When it comes to my investigations, I can tell a lie with the best of them. After all, a detective has to be good at that sort of thing. When it comes to Jim, though, there's no way I could even try to prevaricate. There was no way I'd ever want to. That's the wonderful thing about our relationship: Jim and I are completely honest with each other.

Most of the time.

I smiled in the way I knew from experience made a tingle shoot up his spine, and just to make sure I kept him off guard, I gave him a hello kiss. "I just wondered if you were home, that's all. Nothing wrong with the bride checking on the groom, is there? I wanted to talk to you. About the menu for the reception."

"Uh-huh." It was three weeks before our wedding and Jim was waiting until the exact right moment to get his hair cut so that it would be perfect for our big day. When he nodded, a curl of mahogany-colored hair flopped into his eyes. He pushed it back with one hand, then looped an arm around my waist. "If ye were interested in talking about food, you could have done that at Bellywasher's," he said. "You knew I'd be there all day."

"But . . ." I put my arms around his waist and hooked my fingers behind his back. "You're not at Bellywasher's. You're here, at home. Which means if I wanted to talk to you, I knew I'd have to do it here."

"Aye, but you didn't know I would be here, did you?" Did I say I was the detective? It looks like Jim is pretty good when it comes to noticing details, too. He tugged the cuff of his shirt over his hand, reached around me, and wiped my nose print off the front window. "You're trying to get a look inside the house."

Of course I was.

Oh, how I hated to admit it!

"It's not fair," I wailed, stepping back and out of the circle of Jim's arms. "It's going to be my house, too. I should at least have the right to see what's happening inside." Just in case anything had changed in the time since I last made an attempt to check on the renovations going on inside the house, I stood on tiptoe and tried for another look. Call me paranoid, but I was sure that was why Jim had tacked a bedsheet inside the living room window. The only thing I saw was the pattern of blue and white flowers. My shoulders slumped, and I didn't have to try to sound disappointed. "I should have some say-so when it comes to the renovation."

"You're in charge of the wedding." Jim had said these words to me dozens of times since he'd announced that he was redoing his house in honor of the wedding, and believe me when I say I was not complaining. Not about the renovations, anyway. Jim lives in a wonderful ramshackle house in Arlington's Clarendon neighborhood. He'd bought the house for a song from the elderly woman who'd lived there previously, and since he'd sunk all his money into buying it—not to mention into keeping Bellywasher's open and thriving—there was little he could do in terms of updates. Last I'd seen it, the living room was papered in cabbage roses and violets. The dining room was red. The kitchen had aqua appliances and an avocado countertop. Or was it avocado appliances and an aqua countertop? The fact that I honestly couldn't remember said something about how paranoid I am when it comes to cooking.

Needless to say, I am not a cabbage roses, violets, red, aqua, or avocado kind of girl.

And (just as needless to say) one of the reasons I love Jim is that he realizes it and he's willing to change things to accommodate my tastes.

"But shouldn't I have some say?" I lamented, as if he was following my train of thought.

Jim, ever patient, took me by the shoulders and turned me away from the window. "I'm in charge of the renovations."

"But—"

"Uh!" Like I said, he'd reminded me of our agreement a couple dozen times already, so I guess that gave him every right to shush me. He knew continuing our conversation would get him nowhere so he smoothly changed the subject. "Did ye go get your dress fitted this morning like you were supposed to do?"

"Yes." Was that me sounding so peeved? About what I knew was going to be the happiest day of my life?

I shook off my disappointment and crossed the porch so I could flop down on the front steps. "The dress is beautiful and it fits perfectly."

"But?" Jim sat down beside me.

I sighed. "But Eve is taking this wedding and turning it into a coronation." Jim laughed; I wasn't trying to be funny. I made a face. "I told her just what I told you last fall when we got engaged. I'm not looking for the social event of the season. That's not what this wedding is supposed to be about."

"And I'll tell you what I told you then. If Eve's involved, things are bound to get . . . well . . . involved."

"I should have listened."

"And kept your best friend from being a part of your wedding?"

He was right. He knew it, and so did I. I gave in with as much of a smile as I could produce. "I'd never leave Eve out of the loop. I adore Eve. And besides, she's planned so many of her own weddings, I figured she'd be the perfect one to do all the groundwork. I just never thought . . ."

Jim patted my knee. "You need to stand up to her."

I groaned. "I've done my best. When she wanted that flock of doves—"

"She wanted a flock of doves?"

He turned so pale, I had to laugh. "It was a passing fancy and luckily, it passed quickly. So did the idea about the limo, and the candlelight procession and Doctor Masakazu as ring bearer." I shivered at the very thought of Eve's beloved and incredibly spoiled Japanese terrier being part of the ceremony. "I've reined her in. Honest. But now she's talking champagne toasts and floral bouquets and—"

"Well, there will have to be champagne toasts." Jim made it clear that the subject wasn't open to discussion. "You can't expect me to celebrate the best thing that ever happened to me without a champagne toast or two.

Then"—he wiggled his eyebrows—"I will happily switch to a nice dark and foamy beer."

"It's not the toasts I'm objecting to, it's the silver-plated champagne fountain. And I don't mind flowers. Of course I don't mind flowers at a wedding. But carnations can be just as pretty as orchids, and there isn't room in Belly-washer's for the kind of gigantic floral sprays Eve is talking about. They'd fill the bar and leave no room for guests. And she wants your cousin Fi's children in the wedding, too. All of them!" It's not that I dislike children. In fact, I'd like to have a couple of my own. But I knew Emma, Lucy, Doris, Gloria, Wendy, Rosemary, and Alice all too well. When they stayed with Jim for a couple weeks the previous spring, Eve had taken them under her wing and transformed the girls from hellions into well-behaved young ladies. These days . . . well, without Eve's constant tutoring and with a new little brother to tease, the girls were back to their couch-jumping, sister-pushing, careening-through-the-house selves. I knew this for a fact because Fi and Richard had just moved to the area from Florida and we'd seen them the previous weekend. My head was still pounding.

I sighed, and I knew Jim understood. I'd bet his head was still pounding, too. "That's not the kind of wedding I want. You know that, Jim. I want things to be simple. I just want to concentrate on you. And on being the best wife I can possibly be."

"You're already the best possible person you can be; the wife part shouldn't be so hard." He slipped an arm around my shoulders and gave me a quick hug. "But remember, Annie dear, even when you have the best intentions, things don't always work out the way you planned."

"You're saying I shouldn't expect our wedding to be perfect."

"I'm saying that nothing is perfect. Not weddings, not marriages. Even the ones that look perfect from the outside. Especially the ones that look perfect from the outside!"

I gave him a sloppy kiss on the cheek. "Ours is going to be. I'm going to make sure. Knowing what's happening in the house where I'm going to live would be a good start."

"Oh, no!" Jim threw back his head and laughed. "You won't get around me so easily. Not when it comes to this." He looked over his shoulder toward the closed front door. "Have you not seen Alex since you've been here?"

We were back to talking about everything I couldn't see in the house, and just so he'd know I knew it, I harrumphed. "I can't see anything. Not through the living room window or the kitchen window in the back or even the dining room window."

"The dining room window? The one that's so high off the ground you shouldn't even be trying to look in it?"

I was too offended to be embarrassed. "Your neighbor's tree has this low-hanging branch and—"

"You climbed Mrs. Malone's tree? To try and get a peep into the dining room?" It was Jim's turn to groan. "She's a little old lady. She doesn't need to see you lurking about like that, Annie, and I don't need a bride with her arm in a cast. Besides . . ." His smile was mischievous. "I thought you'd do exactly that. Which is why I had the miniblinds installed in the dining room."

I folded my arms over my chest. "And you keep them closed, too."

"It's my duty." He grinned. "As a husband who wants to please his wife."

"But—"

"No buts." He stopped my objection with a quick kiss. "This is my wedding gift to you and I want it to be special. That means it has to be a surprise."

"But—"

This time, he kissed me longer. Right before he hopped to his feet. "I just stopped home to see what Alex was up to. He didn't answer when I called this morning. I'm going to pop inside and see if he needs any help."

I got to my feet, too. "I could help you find him."

Jim's expression teetered between tolerance and I-can't-believe-you-had-the-nerve-to-say-that. "It's a small enough house that I think I can find him myself, thank you very much." He unlocked the front door. "If I find ye back in that tree . . ." he warned, and he opened the door just enough to slip inside before I could see anything. I wasn't imagining it; I heard the door lock behind him.

There was nothing I could do but wait, so I went back to the steps and sat back down. Now that I thought about it, I was surprised I hadn't heard Alex rambling around in the house while I was trying to get a look inside. Alex is not quiet, especially when he's working. Come to think of it, I hadn't heard the radio he usually played at full blast, either.

The Alex in question was Alex Bannerman, Jim's cousin who had come all the way from Scotland to be the best man at our wedding. Alex was as rough-and-tumble as Jim was quiet and laid-back, a strapping, handsome man of thirty-eight with a shock of hair as red as a Virginia sunset. Alex never talks, he bellows. He doesn't walk, he sprints. Alex believes in taking in life not in tiny bites but in huge gulps, and he proves it by singing too loud, eating all the wrong foods (and still managing to look like a million bucks), and—as he himself admitted the very first time I met him—loving too many women with too much passion to ever make him a successful candidate for marriage.

It was impossible not to like Alex. He was like a big, friendly bear, all smiles and hugs. In fact, the only fault I could find with him was that, like his cousin, he loved to cook. I didn't hold it against him. In fact, I'd become inordinately fond of what he called his "broken biscuit cake," a concoction of chocolate, nuts, and crumbled cookies. So much so, in fact, that I was a little worried about fit when I went to try on my wedding dress that morning.

Alex is also a skilled craftsman. He's a carpenter and a plumber. He's good at painting and hanging wallpaper. There was even talk about him being an expert when it came to laying carpet. As his wedding gift to us, Alex had arrived four weeks earlier and was remodeling Jim's house.

Who could ask for more?

Curious, both as to what Alex had been up to and why he hadn't answered when Jim called him that day, I got up and tried for a look in the front window again, but even before I did, I knew I was wasting my time. When I heard Jim inside, I pretended I was taking a look at the pots of herbs he'd put out on the porch railing to catch the afternoon sun.

"That's a bit daft, isn't it?" Jim wasn't talking about me and the plants. In fact, I'm not sure he even noticed that I was pretending to mess with the rosemary and the mint. He was lost in thought. "Alex isn't here," he said. "I left early this morning. I thought he was still asleep.

But . . ." As if trying to work through it, he shook his head. "His bed isn't slept in. He went out last night and I thought he'd come home after I was already in bed. Apparently not."

"Maybe Alex has met another woman to fall in love with." I was only half kidding.

Jim didn't look convinced. "Maybe. But what if something's happened to him? You don't suppose—"

"Nothing has happened to Alex." I managed to make it sound like I believed it. The last thing either one of us needed to do was to let our imaginations run wild. When they did, more often than not these days, they ran toward murder.

I shook away the thought. "Alex is fine. Alex is always fine. Haven't you said so yourself? Alex is everybody's friend. He doesn't have an enemy in the world. Nobody would ever—"

"There might have been an accident." Thinking about the possibility, Jim's brows dipped low over his eyes. "Or he might have gotten mugged. He could be lyin' in an alley somewhere. He's got only his driver's license and that shows his address back home, and the police wouldn't know he's stayin' here with me, and—"

One hand on his arm, I stopped Jim the way he had stopped me from panicking so many times. "There's no use worrying. Not if we don't know there's anything to worry about. My money's on a woman."

"Aye." Jim nodded. I'm not sure if he was agreeing with me or trying to talk himself into believing I was right. "A woman. It must be. It is Alex, after all!" He smiled in the way I'd seen him smile so many times when he talked about his cousin. Back when Jim still lived in Scotland, he and Alex had a number of wild adventures they'd told me about, and more, I was sure, they hadn't dared to mention. Jim knew his cousin better than anyone, and he knew that Alex would come dragging home soon and work twice as hard the rest of the day to make up for the time he'd lost.

He pulled in a breath and, seeing some of the tension go out of his shoulders, I relaxed. "You're right," he said. "I'm going back to Bellywasher's. We've got crab cakes as a dinner special tonight and that means the place will be full. And when I get home tonight—"

"Alex will be here singing and painting. Or will he be wallpapering?"

"Ye think I'm that easy to dupe?" Jim laughed. He wrapped an arm around my shoulders and together we headed down the steps. "What Alex is doing—"

Before he had a chance to tell me, his cell phone rang. He plucked it out of his pocket. "Maybe we'll find out what Alex is doing. Maybe this is him."

He flipped open the phone and I knew he was right about the call being from Alex because in an instant, the worry was erased from Jim's face. He smiled and gave me the thumbs-up. "I've been worried about ye, man. I was sure something was wrong. But Annie was right. Annie's often right, in case ye haven't noticed. She said—" He stopped for a moment and listened. "What's that?"

It wasn't so much what he said as the tone of his voice that sent a shiver through me. I held my breath and waited to hear more.

"We'll come. Of course we'll come," Jim said. "Right now."

He flipped his phone closed, but in spite of his promise to Alex, he didn't move a muscle. In fact, he stood as still as if he'd been encased in the same ice water that washed through my veins.

Automatically, I reached for Jim's hand "What is it? What's wrong?"

He swallowed hard. "It's Alex," he said. His voice was hollow, his face was suddenly ashen. "He's at the Arlington police station. He's . . ." Jim drew in a long breath and when he let it out, it wobbled over the emotion he could barely control. "Alex has been arrested in connection with a murder."

Two

✖

I WAS NEVER SO HAPPY TO SEE ANYONE AS I WAS to run into Tyler Cooper the moment we were inside the doors of the Arlington Police Department headquarters. Even though Tyler was dating Eve again, he wasn't exactly what I'd call a friend. He was, however, a contact—an official police contact. That was exactly what we needed if we were going to find out what was going on.

I closed in on him before he had a chance to duck and run. "What's going on?" I demanded. "Tyler, what happened?"

He looked from me to Jim, and apparently Tyler decided that Jim was his better bet. Little did he know that Jim loved Alex like a brother. If Tyler was counting on Jim to be either coolheaded or objective, he was in for a surprise. "Your cousin called you?"

"No, we're psychic." Too antsy to keep still and sure poor Alex had been caught up in some red-tape mix-up, I stepped between Jim and Tyler. "Of course Alex called us. How else would we know that you're holding him on some trumped-up charge? Why else would we be here? It's a bureaucratic snafu of epic proportions. It must be. What else would explain it? And what in the world—"

It was Jim's turn to step in front of me, and though I didn't appreciate it, I knew he was justified. I am usually calm and levelheaded, remember. The fact that I was spouting off like that silver-plated champagne fountain Eve wanted at the wedding said something about how much I liked Alex, and how worried I was that he was mixed up in some ugly misunderstanding he needed our help to get out of.

Unlike me, Jim kept his voice low, but still, there was no mistaking the look in his eyes. Another couple minutes of not knowing what was going on, and Jim's head was going to pop. Yeah, like a champagne cork. "Ye've got the wrong man," he told Tyler.

In spite of all the times I claimed otherwise, I know that deep down inside, Tyler really does have a heart. Eve wouldn't love him otherwise. He does not, however, like to show it. Especially in public. Most especially when the public place we were in was the place he worked, and his colleagues were coming and going all around us. After all, Tyler had his reputation as a ruthless jerk to uphold.

Without a word, he turned and walked down a corridor that was less crowded than the main entrance where we'd run into him. It wasn't until we were well out of range of any eavesdroppers that Tyler stopped. He sucked on his lower lip and shook his head sadly. "Your cousin's in a pack of trouble."

"But, Tyler, you know him!" I should have left the talking to Jim. As Alex's contact in the States, it was Jim's responsibility to deal with the authorities in case of a screwup like this. But I couldn't keep my mouth shut. No matter how hard I tried. And I wasn't trying very hard. I knew how quiet Jim had been on the ride over. I saw how stiff his shoulders were, how his jaw was steady and tight. The worry was eating him up, and, seeing Jim worried, I reacted as only a fiancée can. I went on the attack. "You've met Alex. You and Eve and me and Jim and Alex, we all just had dinner together last week. He's fun and he's friendly and—"

"Fun and friendly have nothing to do with this." For a moment, Tyler's expression flashed from sympathetic to stony and I saw the side of him reserved for those who broke the law. It wasn't pretty. "It's not my case," he admitted. "But I heard them talking in the squad room this morning, I heard them mention Alex's name. I don't know all the details . . ."

"But?" Jim stared at Tyler, waiting for more.

One side of Tyler's mouth pulled into up into what was more a grimace than a smile. "From what I hear," he said, "it sounds pretty cut-and-dried. Alex is going to be arraigned, but until he is, he's going to have to stay here."

"In jail?" My stomach soured.

Jim put a hand on my shoulder to steady me. "We can see him?" he asked Tyler, ever the voice of reason, even when it came to something this crazy. "We're allowed to talk to him?"

Tyler seemed to weigh the wisdom of allowing the visit. He gave in with a curt nod. "I know the lead detective on the case. I'll talk to him. I'll get you five minutes. And if anybody asks, it's because Alex is a foreign national and you have to work out how to get him an attorney." He looked my way. "Can you do this without creating a scene?"

"Me? Create a scene? You have got to be kidding! Admit it, Tyler, I'm the most reasonable person you've ever met. I wouldn't create a scene. I wouldn't even know how." It wasn't until I heard my voice echoing back at me and saw a couple people passing by look our way that I realized I already had. I gulped down my mortification, stepped back when I realized I was up in Tyler's face, and nodded, my arms pressed to my sides. "I'll behave," I promised. "Once we get this straightened out . . ."

I was hoping for a little bit of encouragement from Tyler, something like *yeah, you're right, we'll have this straightened out in just a jiffy*. When he didn't say a thing, when he simply pivoted and waved an arm to point us in the proper direction, the acid in my stomach shot into my throat. I clutched Jim's arm and together we walked toward the jail.

Fifteen minutes later, we were standing in a room that contained nothing but a gray metal table and four matching chairs. We were surrounded by a wire cage. There was a guard outside the door. The ambience made it impossible to relax. I paced from the table to the door and back again.

"Sit down." When I walked by, Jim caught my hand and tugged me to a stop. "They're not even going to let Alex walk in if you're looking so edgy; they think you're planning some sort of prison break."

"Do I look like I am?" Heat raced up my neck and shot into my cheeks. "I didn't mean it." I glanced toward the guard at the door. "I didn't mean to look fishy," I said again, a little louder this time, just so he knew I was sincere. I forced myself to breathe, sat—and popped up again in an instant when I saw Alex being led down the hallway by another guard.

The first guard unlocked and opened the door and

Alex stepped inside. I controlled the urge to race over and give him a hug, but only barely, and only because we'd been warned that we were to have no physical contact with what Tyler called "the prisoner." Instead, through the tears that misted my eyes, I looked over the man who was to be the best man in my wedding in just a few short weeks.

Even in prison pants with an elastic waist and a shape-less shirt the exact color of his fiery hair, Alex looked pale. There were dark smudges under his eyes and they were sunken and hollow. He was relieved to see us; I knew because for just a moment, he allowed an anemic smile to brighten his expression. It was gone again in an instant. As if he remembered where he was—and why—Alex's broad shoulders slumped.

He swallowed hard and looked from me to Jim. "I d'na know what to say."

"Just tell us what happened." Jim patted the table across from where he sat. "Sit down, man, and explain what's going on."

Alex did, and once he was seated, I sat down, too. For a couple long, uncomfortable moments, we simply stared at each other, unsure of where to start. But I remembered what Tyler had told us: We had five minutes. I wasn't willing to waste them.

"Tyler says you were picked up in connection with a murder," I said, and three cheers for me, I managed to keep my voice even and unemotional, even though my insides were jumpy. When I realized my hands were shaking, I tucked them in my lap. Alex looked miserable enough, there was no use letting him know the rest of us were worried sick, too. "This has got to be some sort of crazy mix-up. Alex, tell us what happened."

No doubt the police had already asked him to explain

what had happened. It didn't take Alex long to start into his story. "I worked at the house yesterday. Ye know that, Jim. You stopped in and saw what I'd done in the—"

Darn! Though he was wearing prison issue and there was a charge of murder hanging over his head, Alex remembered he was sworn to secrecy when it came to the renovation. If he saw that I'd leaned forward, eager to hear more, he didn't let on. He simply collected his thoughts and started over.

"I worked at the house, I finished up around seven, showered, and went out for a bite."

"Which you know you don't have to do." I suppose it was only natural for Jim to try to hang on to the mundane in the face of something so serious. "There's always food in the fridge, and you could come over to Bellywasher's anytime you want."

Alex expressed his thanks with what was almost a smile. The very effort made him wince, and he got back down to business. "So you've told me a thousand times since I've been here, Jim, but as I've told you, I won't be a leech. Besides, it's good to get out after a long day in the house. There's this place over on Wilson that I've found. Swallows, it's called."

We both knew it well. Jim and I had eaten at Swallows a time or two. He admired the innovative things they did with vegetables. Me? I loved their Baileys chocolate cheesecake. We'd both marveled at the extent of their wine list and their knowledgeable waitstaff.

"On Tuesdays," Alex continued, "they've got Guinness on special and a Celtic band."

Homesickness wasn't Alex's style. I studied him closely. "And women."

"Aye." For once, his eyes didn't sparkle at the prospect. "And not just women. One woman. Her name was Vickie."

I scooted forward in my seat. "And Vickie was at Swallows last night?"

Alex nodded. "The first time I met her . . . well, that was three weeks ago, and as I've told you before, I'm hardly looking for a long-term commitment. Vickie was a pretty thing, and I was looking to have a good time. She came in alone. I bought her a couple drinks, we listened to the music, shared a laugh or two. She left a little after midnight, and I wondered if I'd ever see her again. I went back the next night, but she never showed."

"And last night was Tuesday." I made a mental note of it. "And last night was different how?"

He shrugged. "I arrived near eight, just as I always do. Vickie was already there. She waved to me and I joined her at our usual table."

I picked up on the subtle inference, even if Alex wasn't willing to say it. "Your *usual* table. So you'd seen her there again, after that first time you met her?"

Another nod. "Each Tuesday, sure as eggs is eggs, there was Vickie. And I got to know her. I mean . . ." A touch of color relieved some of the pallor in Alex's face. "She was always a perfect lady and believe it or not, I was as much of a gentleman as I am able to be. You know what I'm saying, Jim." He looked at his cousin. "No hanky-panky. I never saw her anywhere but the bar, and she was a nice woman. A nice, decent woman."

"How old?" It wasn't out of place for me to ask. As I'd learned over the course of four other investigations, every little detail counted, and I never knew which might turn out to be important.

Alex considered the question. "My age, I suppose," he said. "Maybe a little younger, a little older. She was so high." He raised a hand and demonstrated, holding it up about five and a half feet above the green linoleum.

"Yellow-haired, slim. Always nicely dressed. There's another bar in the area, that one where there are always motorcycles parked outside—"

"The Garage." Jim supplied the name of the place.

"That's the one. Vickie, she dinna look as if she'd fit in at a place like that, if you know what I mean," Alex said. "You know, not rough-and-tumble. She dressed neatly, in tailored clothes. Nothing flashy or fancy. You know, like Annie."

Before I could decide if I should take this as a compliment or an insult, Alex went right on.

"She wore a bit of tasteful jewelry now and then. She was a classy lady." He choked over these last words and though I was reluctant to bring up anything that might be painful, I knew I had to keep probing.

"So last night, you walked into Swallows, saw Vickie, and sat down with her. Then . . . ?"

"I ordered a Guinness. She had a chardonnay. Same as usual. She said she wasn't hungry, that she'd had a bite before she left the house. I ordered a steak and artichoke and spinach dip, too, just in case she changed her mind and she wanted something to munch. We chatted and when the band came on—"

"What time?" I asked.

"Nine. Like every other Tuesday. When the band came on, we danced. Vickie, the first night I met her, she said she wasn't much for dancing, but over the last couple weeks, I think I'd changed her mind about that. She actually seemed to enjoy getting out there on the dance floor. When the band took a break, we came back to the table, had another couple drinks, danced again once the music started back up."

As ordinary as he tried to make it sound, I knew there was more to the story than that. There had to be if murder somehow entered the picture. "And that's all?" I asked. "That's all that happened? And it was no different from any other Tuesday?"

Alex shifted uncomfortably in his seat. It was all the answer I needed.

I put my elbows on the table and leaned forward. "You've got to tell us, Alex. No matter what it is. It might be important."

"It's not." He was so sure of himself, I would have let the matter drop—if I hadn't investigated those other murders. I knew better than to let any bit of information slip through the cracks. He, of course, being the normal person he is, thought what he knew—or at least what he thought he knew—was what really happened. Alex was lucky enough never to have been this close to murder before. "We were dancin'," he said, suddenly shy, though shy was the last thing I ever would have called Alex, "and the music was playin' all around me and Vickie's hand was in mine and . . . well, I guess I couldn't help myself. I kissed her."

"And Vickie didn't like that?" It was Jim's turn to ask the questions. I was just as glad. I was doing my best to picture the scene and process everything Alex was telling us. "What did she do?"

"Well, it wasn't exactly as if she didn't like it. She didn't get upset or anything. She laughed, like it was a joke. You know? And then she fanned a hand in front of her face and said she was hotter than blazes and needed to go back to the table for a drink of water."

"You did?" Again, I let Jim take the lead.

"Aye." Alex's hands were on the table, his fingers threaded together. He stared down at them. "Vickie sat down and took a drink. I slipped into the chair next to hers. I tried again to kiss her and she . . ." He was as baffled now by Vickie's behavior as he'd been the night before. "She popped up and said she was ready to start dancing again."

"And so you did." This time, I chimed in. "How long did you dance?"

"Twenty minutes maybe." Alex unwound his fingers and tapped them on the tabletop. "The band took a break and I thought, it was now or never. When we got back to the table, I told Vickie everything I'd been wantin' to say to her. I told her I liked her. A lot. I told her I wasn't satisfied just seeing her there at the bar on Tuesdays. I asked if we could get more serious about each other. You know, if we could date."

Don't ask me how, but I saw where this was going. It was a place I didn't like. "Vickie got mad?"

"As a wet hen!" Even now, he couldn't believe it; Alex shook his head. "The woman not only read me the riot act, she punctuated every word of it with an exclamation mark. She said—"

"That she was just out for a few laughs. That she had no intention of getting serious with you or anyone else. That you should have realized it from the start, and that now that she knew you didn't, she couldn't believe you weren't willing to just back off and forget the whole thing."

Alex looked at me in wonder. "Aye. That's pretty much exactly what she said. How did you know?"

It didn't take a rocket scientist. Or a detective. I explained. "Call it woman's intuition. You tried to kiss her. You told her you liked her. It's pretty obvious the story doesn't have a happy ending. Otherwise, we wouldn't be here. So naturally, I deduced that she freaked, and freaking doesn't make any sense in light of the fact that she was willing to meet you at Swallows every Tuesday. What that tells me is she liked you just as much as you liked her. But she still objected when you asked about dating. So she pulled out every generic excuse in the book, but none of them really explain anything about what she was really thinking or what was really going on."

"You mean excuses like just being out for a few laughs, things like that." Following my logic, Jim nodded. "Is it important?" he asked me.

"Not as important as what Alex did after." I'd been looking Jim's way, and now I turned my attention to Alex. "Was Vickie just sitting there saying all this to you? Or did she get up? Was she standing, like she wanted nothing more than to race out of there?"

"Aye. Exactly." Alex pushed back his chair and stood. He paced over to the far wall. "I tried to reason with her, but she was beyond listening. And as God is my witness, I can't say why. I hadn't said I wanted to run away to Vegas and marry her or anything. I told her only that I thought it would be nice if we saw more of each other. Does that seem such a bad thing?"

It didn't, at least not to me. I wondered why to Vickie it was life and death.

The thought was a sobering reminder that we had yet to hear the whole story.

"I told her she was out of her head," Alex continued. "I asked if she'd had too much to drink perhaps, and she didn't take that well, either. I told her I'd call a cab for her and that I'd accompany her home if she wasn't well. And Vickie . . ." He stared at the blank wall behind us, no doubt reliving the whole ugly scene. "She ran out of the place so fast, I never had a chance to stop her." Alex turned and walked away and his shoulders rose and fell. "I went after her, of course," he said, his voice muffled because his back was to us. "I pushed through the front door and stepped outside. I saw a bus go by. Then . . ." His voice trailed away.

By now, I wasn't just eager to hear the rest of the story, I knew that if we didn't hear it—and fast—we might not have time before the guard came to take Alex back to his cell. I didn't dare get up and walk over to Alex; I didn't want that guard to suspect we were up to anything. Instead, I kept my place and did my best to calm the urgency in my voice. "What happened when you got outside, Alex?" I asked.

"Well, that's the thing." He turned toward us, his expression grim and his face paler than ever. "Inside the restaurant, I remember tryin' to reason with Vickie well enough. I remember how she stormed out of the place and I remember going after her. You know, the front door and the bus. But after that . . ." Alex pounded back to the table and dropped into his chair. "After that, I swear to God I don't remember another thing. Not until this morning. Not until . . ." Again his voice faded, and this time, I knew it would do me no good to egg him on. Alex was dealing with something traumatic. Something ugly. He needed to do it at his own pace.

His hands trembling, he sank back in his chair. "The next thing I remember, there was a police officer's hand on my shoulder and he was shaking me awake. I sat up. I was out in the alley next to the restaurant. And I swear, Jim . . . Annie . . ." He looked from one of us to the other. "I swear I have no memory of how I got there."

I was almost afraid to ask. "And Vickie?"

Alex swallowed so hard, I saw his Adam's apple bob. "I was surprised to see the officer, of course. I didn't know what had happened. I sat up. My head felt as if it was stuffed with wool batting. My mouth was dry. My eyes were bleary, but it didn't take me but another moment to notice there were two more policemen behind the one who helped me to sit up. They had their guns out."

"Because Vickie . . ."

"There were police cars at the mouth of the alley. And more officers." Alex's eyes were bright with tears and, being the manly type he was, I knew he'd never allow that to happen. Not if he wasn't moved by some powerful emotion. He scrubbed his hands over his face. "It wasn't until they'd handcuffed me and moved me off from where they found me that I realized there was blood on my clothing. Lots of it. I felt like hell. I still do. But I wasn't hurt. The blood wasn't mine."

My stomach was so tight, I felt as if a hand had reached inside me and tied it into a couple million painful knots. It was hard to take a breath. When had I reached over and grabbed Jim's hand? I wasn't sure, I only knew I held on tight. "And . . ." The words wouldn't form. I hauled in a lungful of air and tried again. "And Vickie was . . ."

"That's the hell of it." Alex slapped a hand down on the table loud enough to make the guard outside jump. Jim signaled to the man that all was well, and we turned our attention back to Alex. "You know me well enough, Jim. You know I'd never hurt another person. Not for anything in all the world."

"Aye. I know." Jim stared at his cousin, waiting for the rest of the story.

"And I'd know. Don't you think I'd know if I did something like what they're saying I did?" Alex scraped a hand through his hair. "It's daft, that's what it is. It makes no sense. If only I could remember!"

Yes, I'd been told to keep my distance, and keep my hands to myself. And yes (again), I'm all about following rules and regulations. But there are certain situations that defy rules. This was one of them. I couldn't bear to watch Alex suffer and not offer what little support I was able. I darted out a hand to reach across the table and give Alex's hand a squeeze.

The gesture calmed him. "Vickie's dead," he said, his voice as flat as the look in his eyes. "She was there in that alley. They found me a-lying right on top of her. I had . . ." He swallowed hard. "They say I had one of the steak knives from the restaurant in my hand. They say it's the knife I used to kill her."

Three

✖

WHEN STACIE, THE YOUNG LADY WHO'D INTRO- duced herself as our server at Swallows that afternoon, disappeared into the kitchen, Eve took the opportunity to smack her lips. "Baileys chocolate cheesecake. Yum!" It wasn't at all like Eve to be so obvious (at least in public) when it came to how much she enjoyed food, but believe me, I understood.

The Baileys chocolate cheesecake at Swallows is to die for.

Though Eve didn't know what I was thinking, I cringed. *To die for* was a bad expression considering what happened to Vickie at the restaurant.

Rather than think about it, I talked through my logic for this visit with Eve. It was better than staring at the kitchen door, waiting for Stacie and drooling like one of Pavlov's dogs.

"Yes, the cheesecake is fabulous," I admitted. "But remember, it's also a perfect excuse for us to be here." I patted the table we'd found in the corner. It was late on

Wednesday afternoon, and even though Jim was worried about Alex, he was hard at work at Bellywasher's. Jim is a professional, remember. It would take more than an investigation to make him abandon his duties at the pub. After we left police headquarters, Jim asked me to look into what happened, and since I was worried about Alex, too—not to mention how worried I was about what all that worry was doing to Jim—I agreed to take on the case. Naturally, Eve wasn't about to be left behind.

Which made me wonder why she wasn't even listening.

Instead, Eve's eyes took on that glassy look they get when her head's in the clouds and her imagination is getting carried away with it.

"Baileys chocolate cheesecake would be perfect," she crooned, and when I looked at her in wonder, she rolled her eyes. "For the wedding, of course! My goodness, Annie, you've only got three weeks before the big day and you haven't even made a final decision about the cake. Clara's going to need to know. And soon." Clara was a woman who made some of the pastries served at Bellywasher's.

"Clara knows I want simple," I reminded Eve. "She knows Jim and I want to keep the entire wedding low-key."

"But there are details to consider, Annie. Fresh flowers on the cake? A fountain? Oh, a fountain!" Eve's eyes glazed and I thought I'd lost her, but she snapped herself out of it before she could get too carried away on a cascade of fountain daydreams. "Porcelain figures? You know, a bride and groom? It's all important. And you can't know what you're going to do about any of it until you decide once and for all what kind of cake you're having. Chocolate cheesecake, that's one delicious detail!"

"We don't need it." I said this in a way that sounded sincere, even though I am of the mind that everyone *always* needs chocolate cheesecake. I'm pretty sure it's one of the basic food groups. "I had a big, splashy wedding the first time. I'm not making that mistake again."

"The big and splashy part had nothing to do with how things didn't work out between you and Peter," she said, even though she didn't need to point it out. I am nothing if not reasonable. I know the fancy gown and the limo and the flowers and the videographer had nothing to do with the fact that my marriage to Peter had gone ker-flooey. That had happened thanks to the girl Peter met at the dry cleaner's—and the undeniable fact that Peter is a weasel. "That doesn't mean you shouldn't do big and splashy again," Eve added.

"No." I was as clear as I could be. It didn't pay to beat around the bush with Eve. "We're keeping it simple. That's why we're having the ceremony and the reception right at Bellywasher's. No big church extravaganza. No reception it's going to take us three years to pay off. Simple ceremony. Simple foods. I can't expect Marc and Damien to spend the evening in the Bellywasher's kitchen cooking when they should be enjoying the party. That's why I've been thinking . . ." The idea had just occurred to me in the middle of the night before, and I hadn't had a chance to run it by Eve yet. Excited, I leaned forward.

"I want to cook something special for Jim," I told her. "You know, to serve at the wedding."

Can I blame her for looking incredulous? I cannot. Even so, I found myself feeling a little offended.

"Hello, Annie!" Eve waved a hand in front of my face. "You and cooking? You don't exactly get along. Remember the exploding stove? And the burned-beyond-belief chicken wings? And the—"

"Which is why it's such a great idea." Yes, I am ever practical, but apparently, when it comes to love, even the most practical woman can get a little crazy. I'd made up my mind and nothing was going to change it. Not even the thought of going near a stove and (gulp!) turning it on.

"It would be a total and complete surprise for Jim," I said, convinced.

"Yeah, Bellywasher's burning down on your wedding day. That ought to do it."

I forgave her the sarcasm. After all, she was right.

And I was so enamored of the idea, I was beyond being able to listen to reason!

I scooted forward on my chair. "I was thinking I'd make some traditional Scottish dish. You know, like—" Since I hadn't had the chance to give it much thought and I wasn't familiar with any traditional Scottish dish beyond the biscuit cake Alex had made for me, I was stumped.

"Oatmeal?" Eve suggested.

Do I need to point out that I was thinking of something a little more upscale and a little less breakfasty?

I pretended to consider the idea anyway. Just so I didn't hurt Eve's feelings. "I'm going to look online," I told her. "I'm thinking it should be something I can make at home. Then I'll smuggle it into the restaurant the day before the wedding, and have Marc and Damien serve it. It will knock Jim's socks off."

I knew better than to respond to the slow upward slide of Eve's eyebrows. She was thinking that if it was anything like my usual cooking, it might knock Jim's socks off, all right. Literally.

"I'm going to try really hard this time," I said, defending myself, though I knew I didn't have to. Eve understood. That's what best friends are for. "I'm going to practice until I can make whatever it is I'm going to make absolutely perfectly. You'll see. It's going to be fabulous."

It was another reason Eve is my best friend. She actually believes me when I say things like that. She propped an elbow on the table and cradled her head in one hand. "You think there might be a traditional Scottish recipe for chocolate cheesecake?" she asked. "That would be fun."

"There's more to fun than cheesecake," I told her. I actually might have believed it if Stacie didn't walk out of the kitchen at that moment. She headed back our way—two pieces of delectable cheesecake poised on the tray in her hands—and I realized there were pluses even to murder investigations. I was at Swallows without Jim for the first time ever. I didn't have to share my cheesecake.

I actually might have enjoyed pigging out if I didn't keep thinking about Alex and how miserable he looked when we said our good-byes at the jail.

When Stacie set our pieces of cheesecake in front of us, I signaled to Eve to keep the oohing and aahing to a minimum so I could do what we'd come to Swallows to do in the first place. (Which was not—just in case I need to point it out—to eat Baileys chocolate cheesecake.)

"So . . ." My fork poised above the drizzle of dark chocolate that made a fancy, curlicue *B* on top of the cake, I looked up at the college-age girl with pitch-dark pigtails. "Is this where the murder happened?"

Stacie closed her eyes for a moment. No doubt she was praying for patience. "That's all anybody can talk about today," she said, and I bet her bosses were as tired of hearing about it as Stacie was, because she kept her voice down and looked toward the woman standing behind the hostess station before she said anything else. I didn't need to work in a restaurant to know that Stacie had been instructed to keep talk of what had happened there the night before to a minimum. After all, murder is bad for business. She sighed. "Everybody who comes in here today is asking about the murder."

"Well, you have to admit, it is pretty interesting," Eve blurted out, and I blanched because, let's face it, when most people think of murder, they think of words like *disgusting* or *frightening* or *horrific*. But then, most people haven't been embroiled in as many investigations as we have. The next second, I thought about Alex, about how pale and anxious he was when last I saw him. I'd bet my piece of cheesecake he didn't think Vickie's murder was *interesting*.

"What Eve meant," I said, giving her a long look so she could pretend to be repentant, "is that it's such a shame. We've been here a few times before and we never thought . . ." As if I hadn't taken a long, hard look around when I walked in—and believe me, I had—I took a long, hard look around. Swallows wasn't nearly as quaint or as cozy as Bellywasher's, and I didn't like it nearly as much, but then, when it comes to Bellywasher's, I'm more than a bit prejudiced. Still, Swallows is a pleasant enough place. Its walls are painted a minty green that's perfect with the oak floors. It has a wide front window that looks out over the street, clean, modern lines, and a sleek bar that takes up all of the wall opposite from where we sat. There's a tiny stage just inside and to the left of the front door and a dance floor in front of that.

"Never in a million years would I think this was the kind of place where a murder would happen," I said.

"Well, it didn't exactly happen here. Not right inside," Stacie said. "The police found the woman's body out there." She tipped her head in the direction of the alley we'd tried to check out before we walked in. Since there was crime scene tape draped between Swallows and the building next door and a uniformed police officer making sure no one crossed it (not even Eve, who did her best to charm him into making an exception), we didn't get very far.

"They found a suspect, too, right? That's what we heard on the news." I'd coached Eve on the way over, and she played her part perfectly. She didn't have to pretend to sound horror-struck, but she did manage to make it seem as if she'd never been so close to a murder before. "The woman's body was out in the alley, and so was the guy who they think killed her. You must have been so scared when the cops showed up!"

"My shift doesn't start until eleven," Stacie said. "I wasn't here when it all went down. From what I heard, there was a whole lot of blood."

Just thinking about it made me second-guess my cheesecake. I didn't want to ask for details, but I had to. Sure, it's my nature to be thorough, but let's face it, there were other things to consider. I knew Alex, and I was certain he wasn't a violent man. More importantly, I knew Jim, and with all his heart, Jim believed Alex was innocent. If Alex's word meant that much to Jim, then it meant that much to me, too. All I had to do to make everyone happy and ensure justice was done was prove that Alex wasn't the killer.

With that in mind, I knew I couldn't trust Eve to ask all the right questions. I took over. "So you weren't here when the cops arrived," I said, reinforcing the information Stacie had already given us. "But somebody was, right? Somebody actually saw it? The body? And the blood? And the guy they arrested?"

"He didn't exactly see it." Stacie looked over her shoulder at the bar. The only employee over there was the bartender, so I knew that was who Stacie was talking about. She bent close enough for me to get a good look at the tattoo on her neck. It was the Tasmanian Devil. "Truth be told, Jason didn't even know anything was going on until he saw the police cars outside. At least that's what he told all of us when we came in. But Jason's pretty slick when it comes to getting tips. He knows that the better the story he tells, the more people will drink, and the more they drink . . ." Stacie made a face. "We're supposed to pool our tips and share them at the end of the shift. But I've seen Jason over there. He's talking up a storm and customers are slipping him money. He puts it right in his pocket. Every time he tells the story, he adds more detail and he makes it sound more gruesome. By the time tonight rolls around, he'll claim he was there watching when the guy slit that woman's throat."

Both Eve and I had wedges of cheesecake on our forks. We didn't need best-friend ESP to think the exact same thing. Two bodies with one mind, we set down our forks. While Eve took a big gulp from the cup of coffee in front of her, I cleared the sour taste from my throat and said, "So Jason didn't even know the body was there. Don't you think someone would have noticed?"

Stacie shook her head. "Nobody ever uses that alley. The kitchen door leads out back, not into the alley. That alley doesn't even go anywhere. I guess it used to, before they built those condos back on Ninth Street. Now the alley's just a dead end."

"But someone must have known the body was there." It was the first time the idea occurred to me, and I threw Eve a look to signal her that it might be important at the same time I wished I'd thought to ask Tyler about it. "If nobody uses the alley, how did the cops find the body in the first place?"

Stacie's shoulders rose and fell, and when the hostess looked our way, she grabbed a nearby coffeepot and pretended to refill my cup. I had a feeling she wasn't as worried about the hostess finding out what we were talking about as she was about being accused of loafing. "All I know is what I heard when I got here. Jason gets here early to stock the bar and make sure everything's ready for the day. He didn't have a clue that anything was wrong. Not until the cops pulled up outside. When they did, he went out and took a look. He's the one who said that stuff. You know, about all the blood."

"Wow." I pretended to think about what she said, but I didn't have to think long. I knew exactly what I wanted to ask next. "They were in here together last night, right? That's what I heard. You heard it, too, didn't you, Eve, on the TV news you watched this morning? We heard that the victim and the suspect ate dinner here together last night."

Stacie had stalled as long as she could. Another look from the hostess and she replaced the coffeepot and stepped back from the table. "I couldn't say. I'm only here during the day."

She walked away, and really, what choice did we have but to finish every last bite of that cheesecake? If we didn't, we would look suspicious. Then again, it seemed Eve and I weren't the only ones at Swallows interested in the murder. Just as we finished up, a camera crew from Channel 4 arrived and set up outside. While everyone else in the small post-lunch crowd concentrated on the news crew, we left a nice-sized tip for Stacie to share with her fellow employees, sauntered over to the bar, and sat down.

Jason ran a bar cloth over the counter in front of us. "What, you two gonna wash down your cheesecake and coffee with a shot or two?"

I excused the sarcasm. He'd already seen us talking to Stacie, so there was no use pretending we were there just for the cheesecake. "I hear you were the first one in here this morning."

Even though neither of us asked for it, he poured two glasses of ice water and set them down in front of us. "You're reporters."

I took a sip—and ignored the question. "You were here when the cops arrived. You saw the body. What I don't understand is how anybody knew the woman was there in the first place. That alley's a dead end."

Jason looked over to where Stacie was delivering beers to another table. "Stacie has a big mouth."

"She didn't say anything that wasn't true. But that's not why you care, is it? You don't want her telling the story because then you won't have a chance to tell it. And to collect some big, fat tips in the process." I propped my elbows on the bar and leaned forward. "You'd better tell me everything. You know, before Stacie spoils it for you. At least if you tell us, we'll know we're getting our information straight from the only person who was here when it happened."

"I wasn't here. Not when it happened."

I had to control myself or I would have rolled my eyes. When it comes to murder, people are so literal. "I didn't mean in the alley," I explained. "I meant here. In the restaurant. Did you work last night?"

"I didn't see a thing. I was too busy pouring Guinness all night."

"And the guy they think killed the victim, did you pour for him?"

I wasn't done with it, but Jason whisked my glass away. "I don't pay any attention to where the drinks are going. I don't have the time. The waitresses give me their orders and—"

"So if a waitress served them, they weren't here at the bar, they were sitting at a table." This fit with what Alex had told me. I scanned the restaurant, wondering which table was Vicki and Alex's *usual*. "It wasn't their first time here. They came every Tuesday."

"And every Tuesday, we're slammed."

I was getting nowhere fast and nowhere wasn't where I wanted to be. A man down at the other end of the bar signaled to Jason for a refill on his scotch, and I waited as patiently as I was able. With no cheesecake to nibble and no one to talk to, I felt self-conscious. There was a stack of Swallows coasters in front of the seat to my right and I grabbed one. I didn't have to pretend to be interested in it. It was an attractive advertising piece, round and made of heavy cardboard, just a little bigger than the bottoms of the glasses stacked neatly behind the bar. It featured a sepia-toned photo of the sign that hung above the front door. The coasters were eye-catching, cheap souvenirs. I had no doubt many a patron left with one.

Once a business manager, always a business manager: I showed the coaster to Eve before I slipped it in the pocket of my jacket. "I just wonder. That's all. I wonder how much they cost per thousand."

By the time Jason came back, I was ready to steer our conversation in another direction. With any luck, Stacie was right, and he'd be more forthcoming when it came to making it sound like he was at the center of the morning's excitement.

I caught Jason's eye. "Stacie tells me you saw what happened this morning."

"I might have." He glanced down at the empty bar in front of me.

And I got the message.

I reached into my purse, fished out a twenty, and set it on the bar. Frugal business manager that I am, I kept my fingers on it. After all, I was paying for information. And so far, I wasn't getting much of anything from Jason.

"The man who was arrested—"

"Drunk as a skunk. Even this morning." Suddenly more talkative, Jason glanced briefly at the twenty before he returned his gaze to me and Eve. "When the cops tried to walk him to the patrol car, he couldn't even stand up. They had to call an ambulance."

This tallied with what Alex had said. He said he didn't remember anything that happened after he ran out of the restaurant after Vickie. If he'd been that drunk . . .

That didn't tally with what I knew about Alex. He liked a beer or two or three. But in the weeks I'd known him, I'd never seen him drunk.

"They say there was a knife in his hands." Eve must have known I was lost in thought. That's why she asked the question.

"Obviously not when I saw him." Jason glanced at the money again before he looked toward three women who'd walked in the door. They were loaded with shopping bags and I heard them say something about martinis. I knew Jason had to take care of the paying customers before he worried about the nosy ones, so I had to move fast.

"How did the police know the body was there?" I asked him.

Jason grabbed one bottle of gin and one of vodka. "I heard one of the cops say something about an anonymous tip."

That might be helpful. It might not. I filed it away for future consideration and drummed my fingers against the twenty. "Who worked the tables last night?"

"Jennifer does an extra shift on Tuesday nights."

"And Jennifer is . . . ?"

He glanced over to where a platinum-haired waitress with a nose piercing had finished taking an order and was walking toward the kitchen.

Just before I popped up to follow her and signaled Eve to come along, I slipped my hand off the twenty.

Surprise, surprise! Jason, it seemed, was something of a magician as well as a bartender. The money disappeared in a flash.

So did we. While the door that led into the kitchen was still swinging, Eve and I slipped inside. We were just in time to see Jennifer go out the back door, and before anybody even noticed us, much less had time to stop us, we followed her outside.

By the time we got there, she was already angled against the back wall of the restaurant, lighting a cigarette.

"You worked last night. You waited on Vickie, the woman who got killed."

Something told me it wasn't the first time that day that Jennifer had been singled out. That's why she wasn't surprised by us or by what I was talking about. No doubt I'd see her quoted in the next day's newspaper, or on TV that night. She naturally assumed Eve and I were just part of the army of reporters who had already talked to her that day. She pulled in a lungful of poison and before she let a stream of smoke out of her mouth, she turned her head away. I liked Jennifer already.

"Waited on them every Tuesday. I thought they were a cute couple."

"But not last night."

Jennifer flicked ash off the end of her cigarette. "Nothing seemed strange to me. Not until right before the woman ran out of here."

I was getting good at picking up on nuances. "Alex didn't drink more than usual?" I asked.

"Alex? Oh, the red-haired guy. Yeah, you're right. I remember a couple weeks ago, he told me that was his name. He was really nice and really funny. I didn't think—" Beneath a heavy coating of blush too orange for Jennifer's pale complexion, she blanched, and I knew I had to get her back on track before she was derailed by the emotional strain of knowing a murdered woman and the man who supposedly killed her.

"He was drunk." It wasn't a question, but still, I hoped she'd answer.

She pulled on her cigarette for a couple long moments before she said, "I didn't think so. I mean, I wouldn't have served him if I thought he was. It's against company policy. Did he have a couple pints? Sure. I delivered his last Guinness just as he and that Vickie woman were getting up to dance. But hell, I'd seen him drink more than that on some nights and still leave here as sober as a judge. He's a big guy. He can hold his liquor. And he seemed fine to me. Right up until the very end, anyway."

Jennifer's cigarette was almost gone and I knew when it was, she'd have to get back on the floor. I didn't wait to ask my next question. "What happened right at the end?"

"Well, they had a fight. I didn't catch exactly what was going on, but . . ."

"But?"

Someone in the kitchen called out to Jennifer that the two bowls of clam chowder she was waiting for were ready. She took another long drag on her cigarette, dropped the butt, and ground it under the sole of her black work shoe. "Vickie said something about him not understanding and trying to push her when she didn't want to be pushed."

This meshed with what Alex had told us about how he'd confessed to Vickie that he wanted to date her and that Vickie had reacted badly. "And when Vickie said that, what did Alex say?"

"Well, that's when he said he wished she was dead."

The news hit me somewhere between my heart and my stomach, and for a while, all I could do was stare at Eve. Since she was staring right back at me, I guess she knew exactly how I felt. It wasn't until I realized I was wasting precious seconds that I forced myself to speak. "He said—"

"'I wish you were dead.' Yeah, that was it. I mean, at least I think it was. The music was kind of loud." Jennifer turned to go back into the kitchen.

I stopped her with one last question. "Do you think Alex could have been drugged?"

It was Jennifer's turn to be shocked, but she was a good sport. She thought about it for a minute. "I had a friend that happened to in a bar over in Reston," she finally said. "Creep who slipped something into her drink tried to get her into his car, but a couple of us, we saw her leaving with him and we knew something was wrong. It's scary, but yeah, you hear it happening to women all the time. But why would somebody drug a guy?"

It was a good question and, convinced it was important to find the answer, we thanked Jennifer and I called Tyler as soon as we stepped out of Swallows and were out of range of that news crew.

"Why am I not surprised you're all over this murder like flies at a Sunday picnic?" he asked.

I didn't take it personally. I mean, I did, but I didn't let

Tyler know it. Again, I asked what I'd asked the second he picked up his phone. "Is it possible Alex might have been drugged?"

Tyler thought about it before he said, "Anything's possible."

"He says anything's possible," I told Eve in a stage whisper before I spoke again in a normal tone of voice. "And you could find out, right? If you did some kind of blood test or something?"

"Paramedics drew blood. Procedure. But don't get your hopes up. Those party drugs are hard to find after they've been in the system more than a couple hours, and nobody looks for them as part of any of the standard tests. You think it's possible?"

"I think it explains why Alex can't remember what happened after Vickie ran out of the restaurant."

"If he's telling the truth."

No, Tyler couldn't see me, but that didn't mean I didn't react to his accusation. My shoulders shot back. "Alex isn't the type of man who lies."

"Which type is that, Annie? The type who's trying to save his butt after he gets caught red-handed? If you're going to play detective, you'd better learn not everybody is what they seem."

"Alex is." I was certain of it. Jim wouldn't be his friend otherwise. Rather than argue with Tyler and get nowhere, I decided to stay with the tried-and-true. Nothing appeals to a cop like logic. "If he is telling the truth, then he could have been drugged, right?"

"If there are drugs involved—and this is a big if, remember—I think it's more likely Alex intended to give them to Vickie."

It was the second time that afternoon that I felt as if I'd been knocked for a loop. Since we were out on the sidewalk, I stepped over to the side to stay out of the way of other pedestrians so I didn't get bowled over, and I motioned to Eve to stand aside, too. She, however, wasn't paying attention. There was a pricey boutique next door and Eve had her eye on a green cocktail dress with skinny straps and a neckline cut down to there.

I left her at it and collected my thoughts. When I didn't make any sense of what Tyler was saying—when I couldn't—I stammered, "What on earth are you talking about, Tyler? Why would Alex want to drug Vickie? He admitted that he liked her, that he wanted to get more serious with her."

"Uh-huh." I could picture Tyler sitting at his desk. When he sat back, I heard his chair squeak. "But what Alex didn't bother to mention was that Vickie wasn't just Vickie. She was Vickie Monroe, Mrs. Edward Monroe."

"She was married?"

"Married? Oh, yeah. And from what her husband said when he came in to identify the body—poor bastard— happily married. They live up in McLean. I can pretty much place the address. It's one of those nice homes in an upscale development. Nice husband, too. He's the owner of some hotshot company up that way. You see what I'm getting at here, Miss Annie the Detective? Home, husband, two little kids, too, by the way. Vickie was a member of the PTA at their school. She volunteered with her little girl's Girl Scout troop. She was a member of the local garden club. She took cooking classes with her friends." He let me digest this information before he added, "Sounds like Vickie Monroe had a nice life, so if your friend Alex was looking to take things to the next level, I can see why Vickie wasn't all that thrilled about having it ruined by a guy she met once a week for a couple laughs. And if Vickie refused, Alex might have—"

"No. It's not possible."

Tyler chuckled. Not like it was funny, like he expected me to argue and he wasn't disappointed. "When you've done this as long as I have, you know that anything and everything is not only possible, it happens all the time."

"But—"

"When you get some real evidence, something we can actually verify, give me a call," he said, and because he didn't expect that to happen anytime soon, he hung up.

I stood there on the sidewalk, trying to make sense of everything he'd told me, and when that didn't work, I waited for Eve to join me and tried to fit the information I had into what I did know about the case.

"Listen to this," I said. "And help me make sense of it all. Alex was found, passed out, with a knife in his hands, with Vickie's body."

There was no denying any of this. Eve nodded. "Ugly but true."

"Yeah, but wait." I held up a hand to let her know I wasn't done. "Tyler says Vickie Monroe was from McLean, one of those ritzy suburbs the two of us always fantasize about."

Eve couldn't deny this, either. Once in a while, back in the day before we both got jobs at Bellywasher's and got so busy, we used to take drives through some of the suburbs we fantasized about. Yes, in our weaker moments, both Eve and I had imagined ourselves living Vickie's life. We'd have perfect homes in a perfect gated community, and of course, we'd be neighbors. My brighter-than-average children would attend the better-than-normal schools nearby with Eve's. Because our husbands would make enough money to support us in the upper-class style we were used to, neither of us would have to work. But that didn't mean we'd be couch potatoes. Both of us would be involved in our kids' lives, and in their activities. Together, Eve and I would contribute to our community.

I came out of the dream when I heard myself sigh. "Oh, yeah," I said, "Vickie Monroe had our dream life, Eve. Well . . ." I flinched. "Except for those cooking classes. And . . ." This time, even a flinch wasn't enough to register my horror. I felt the blood drain from my face. "She had a perfect life except for the cooking classes, and the murder."

Four

✕

BELIEVE ME, I HAD A PLAN. AT LEAST A PLAN AS FAR as my investigation went. I had to wait until the medical examiner released Vickie Monroe's body, but after that, I had every intention of attending her funeral. After all, everybody goes to a funeral: family, friends, neighbors, loved ones. Maybe even murderers. Oh, yeah, I would be there, too, and talking to everyone unfortunate enough to get too close to me.

Until then, I had other things to keep me busy. There was all the work I had to do at Bellywasher's, of course. As business manager at the restaurant, I'm responsible for keeping all our invoices in order, paying our bills, balancing deliveries against receipts against those invoices. I make sure we order the supplies we need and I take care of our bank transactions every single day. I handle payroll, too, as well as things like making sure what we're charging for food actually covers the cost of the food, the preparation, and that payroll. If we're lucky, we can manage a smidgen of profit in there, too.

Yes, in my real job, I do all those wonderful, mundane things other people hate to do, and I love every minute of it. After all, I get all the excitement I need from murder. And from planning my wedding.

These days, it seemed as if the two things had a way of getting all mixed up.

Which was why on Thursday evening, I spent some time at the restaurant thinking about what I could do for Alex and how I'd proceed with my investigation. But once Bellywasher's closed and I kissed Jim good night, Eve and I hurried over to the apartment that wouldn't be my apartment for too much longer. This time, we were investigating—

"Cullen Skink?" I was sitting at my computer, and Eve was standing behind me. She leaned over my shoulder and pointed at the screen, reading out loud. "What on earth is it? And do you really think you'd want to serve something called Cullen Skink at your wedding?"

I wasn't about to so easily dismiss anything that fell under the heading of Scottish cuisine. I clicked around the Internet site I'd found that promised to reveal the secrets of Scots food in all its glory. Or not.

"It's fish soup," I told Eve, speed-reading the page as I went. "And it doesn't sound half bad. You need a smoked haddock, onions, milk, potatoes. I might actually be able to do this!" I grinned at the prospect until I got to the part of the recipe that said *Method*. Then I read aloud and my shoulders drooped. "The first thing you have to do is skin the haddock."

"Oh, my Lord, Annie! We can't have you doing that on your wedding day. You'll smell fishy!"

Eve didn't have to argue to convince me. With my mouse, I zoomed around the page, looking for other suggestions. "Here's one." I stopped and pointed it out. "I don't know what it is, but it sure sounds Scottish. Crappit heid."

She leaned closer and read, "It's the head of a fish stuffed with oats, suet, and the fish liver. It's boiled in seawater. Annie, you're not actually thinking—"

"No." I went back to Google and tried a different Scottish cooking site.

"How about that one?" Eve stopped me with her question. "Black pudding. That's got to be like chocolate pudding, right? And what could be better or easier than chocolate pudding? Oh!" She shivered with delight at the very thought. "We could top it with dollops of fresh whipped cream and strawberries. Wouldn't that be the best?"

It would have been, if black pudding was what we thought it was. The recipe proved otherwise. "It's sausage made by cooking blood with filler until it's congealed," I told Eve, and she didn't wait for me to read more. She grabbed the mouse and clicked off the page.

I was not to be deterred, even in the face of culinary adversity. I kept looking, and my efforts were rewarded. "Here's one that's traditionally served at weddings. It's called cranachan. It's made with whipped cream, whiskey, honey, and fresh raspberries and the whole thing is topped with toasted oatmeal." I didn't wait for her to say yea or nay. I didn't need to. I knew that any recipe that included whipped cream and fresh raspberries was as all right by Eve as it was by me. I had the recipe printed out in a moment, and a few minutes later we were in the kitchen, giving it a whirl.

And I suppose since I've said this much about it, I really should report the results.

Only, do I have to?

Let's just say that by the time it was all over, I had honey stuck in my hair, there was cream (whipped and unwhipped) splattered across the kitchen cabinets, and Eve, who had volunteered to toast the oatmeal in a frying pan, was sitting at my kitchen table with her right hand wrapped in a cold, wet washcloth. The better to keep the blisters down.

It was a good thing my limited supply of at-hand food didn't include fresh raspberries. It would have been a shame to sacrifice fresh raspberries for something that turned into that big a mess.

I sank down on the chair across from Eve's and groaned, and Eve, though she was surely in pain, never forgot that it is the duty of a best friend to boost her best friend's spirits. She knew where I kept supplies for just such an emergency. She got up, fetched the step stool I kept in the kitchen because I'm too short to reach most of my cupboards, and dragged it over to the shelves above the refrigerator. She's tall, but even she had to stretch to reach my emergency supply of giant-sized Hershey bars. That's the idea, of course. If the chocolate is out of reach, I will be less likely to reach for it. Except in the most dire of emergencies.

Eve brought one over along with a jar of extra-crunchy peanut butter and handed me a spoon. "Don't worry. We'll find something that's easy and tastes good, too. You'll still be able to surprise Jim."

I spooned up some peanut butter and coated a square of chocolate with it. I chewed and swallowed it down. "That's the problem," I said, my words sticking to the roof of my mouth. "My bad cooking is exactly what *won't* surprise Jim."

* * *

"I'M THINKING EMMA AND LUCY WOULD LOOK sweet in rose. Not anything mauvy, a true, rosy pink. That way, Doris and Gloria could wear a nice, fresh shade of green. Wendy and Rosemary . . . well, with their coloring, bright yellow might be too much. But then, they're kids, and kids can get away with anything and still look adorable. So let's put Wendy and Rosemary in yellow, but a nice soft shade. That leaves Alice, and I'm picturing lilac for her. And I know, I know, Annie . . ." Even if I hadn't known her forever, I would have picked up on the frustration in Eve's voice. This was a subject she'd brought up time and again for the last . . . oh, I don't know . . . maybe twenty-five years. "I know you aren't into lots of color or flashy fabrics, but you know you really should give it a chance sometime. You know, spread your artistic wings and fly. But really, I mean, this is a wedding and wouldn't it just be adorable if the girls looked like a bouquet of flowers! And Alice's lilac dress will match Little Ricky's bow tie and cummerbund."

Believe me, when Eve gets like this—all talky and making plans so big, all of Virginia can't hold them—I try my best not to fall under her spell. I tried even harder that next Monday morning as we sat in Willburger's Funeral Chapel waiting for the service for Vickie to begin. For one thing, this was hardly the place to talk about a wedding. For another, it wasn't the time, either, considering that we were attending the funeral so we could find out all we could about Vickie and—if we were lucky—so we could find someone who might be responsible for her death. Someone other than Alex, that is.

At least Eve knew enough to keep her voice to a whisper. That was a plus. So was the fact that we were sitting in the last row of folding chairs, back near a credenza filled with photographs of Vickie and her family, a vase with two dozen yellow roses in it, and a box of tissues I had a feeling I was going to need as soon as Edward Monroe and his kids walked in.

Funerals always do that to me.

I was doing my best not to get sucked in by Eve's wild plans, but I was looking for a distraction. Desperate to think about anything other than that urn sitting on a table at the front of the room, what was in it, and why, I turned to Eve. "Little Ricky's wearing a cummerbund?"

"Well, of course." For a second, Eve forgot where we were, and her voice was a tad too loud. She hushed it. "Ricky has to wear a cummerbund with his little tuxedo. Who even knew they made tuxes for one-year-olds! My goodness, Annie, but he's going to look as cute as a button! And so are his big sisters, of course. A bouquet of flowers. Don't you just love thinking of those darling little girls that way?"

There was a flurry of activity outside the big double doors that led into the room. I could hear the respectful murmur of voices. The reminder of where we were and why brought me to my senses. "The kids aren't going to be in the wedding," I told Eve. My voice might be no more than a whisper, but there was no mistaking that I meant what I said. "I've told you before, Eve. It's not that I don't like the kids, it's just that I don't want this wedding to turn into a three-ring circus."

Her shoulders drooped. Not like mine do when I'm disappointed. When I'm disappointed, I fold up like an origami stork and that makes me look shorter than ever. When Eve expresses her disappointment . . . well, I swear, even droopy shoulders didn't detract from the perfect drape of her white cashmere sweater. She sank back into the chair and crossed her incredibly long legs.

"You're ruining all my fun," she harrumphed below her breath.

"It's not a trip to an amusement park, it's a wedding. And in case you've forgotten, it's my second wedding. We went through all the rigmarole the first time."

That was enough to make her forget her disappointment. Eve sat up like a shot. She controlled herself, but just barely. "Oh, wasn't it fabulous, that first wedding of yours! Remember the cake, Annie? You wanted that plain ol' nothing of a wedding cake and I canceled the order and didn't tell you. And when they carried in the five-tiered cake with the fresh flowers and the streamers and the sparklers . . ."

I remembered, all right. Every once in a while the feeling of mortification that had rooted me to the spot in the middle of the dance floor still pops up in my nightmares. Before it got the best of me, I knew it was wise to shake away the memory. "We've got bigger things to worry about than the wedding," I reminded Eve.

Thinking about it, she glanced around at the somber-faced people around us. "Do you think the real killer is here?"

"I know the real killer isn't back in the Arlington jail." I looked around, too. In the fifteen minutes since we'd arrived, the room had gone from empty to just about full. Sad-eyed men in dark suits sat side by side with women who dabbed tissues to their noses. Near us at the back of the room were a couple women who we'd learned from eavesdropping were teachers at the Monroe children's school. In front of them was a man who'd turned to them at one point and introduced himself as the Monroe family financial planner. As is usual at funerals, the folks nearest to the front of the room were also nearest and dearest to the deceased. Everybody who walked in stopped to console an elderly couple, and I pegged them as either Vickie's parents or her father- and mother-in-law. The man in the gray suit who was holding a Bible was the minister who would conduct the service. It was the women sitting in the front row and all the way to the right who interested me most. There were three of them, and at the same time I wondered if Vickie had sisters, I knew these were probably not relatives.

They were all about my age and since that was about Vickie's age, too, I decided they must be Vickie's closest friends. The first was a tiny, attractive Asian woman in a trim black pantsuit. Soon after she walked in, I heard someone address her as Celia. Next to Celia was a taller, heavyset woman in a dress the exact shade of her filmy gray eyes. She had corn-colored hair and a complexion so pale, she looked like a ghost in a Syfy Channel show. Celia called the pale lady Glynis. Next to Glynis was Beth, a pretty woman of about my height, with shoulder-length brown hair and eyes that were red and swollen from crying. She was wearing a black skirt and a white blouse with tiny white flowers embroidered all over it. There was an empty chair in between each woman and when the double doors opened, three men who'd been talking quietly together in the hallway took their places at their wives' sides.

Celia's husband was tall and as skinny as a string bean. Glynis's was short and round. Beth's reminded me of a cartoon caricature, a sort of nebbish with a bland expression, thick glasses, and a bald spot that reflected the dim overhead lights.

When a representative from the funeral chapel walked in, an expectant silence fell over the crowd. Beth got a handkerchief out of her purse. Celia grabbed her husband's hand. Glynis dropped her head on her husband's

shoulder and began to sob. I almost started, too, when a
man in a black suit who I knew must be Edward Monroe
walked in. He was still in shock from the horror of what
had happened to his wife, and he had one arm around a
little girl of eight or so and a hand atop the head of a five-
year-old boy.

I had to look away so my heart wouldn't break. "It's
not possible," I mumbled to myself, but I was sure Eve
heard. "There's no way Alex could have caused this
much sadness."

I had the next twenty minutes or so to think about it
while the minister read a passage from the Bible, and a
man who introduced himself as Noel, Vickie's brother,
talked about their growing-up years. He had finished
going through their elementary school days, year by
year, and started on their middle school years when Eve
leaned over.

"Do you really think he could have been drugged?"

For a moment, I thought she was talking about Noel,
who was certainly putting the rest of us to sleep with
details about his life and very little useful or interesting
about Vickie. I shook myself out of my Noel-induced
stupor and remembered that Eve and I had talked on
our way to McLean about the possibility of someone
slipping something in Alex's drink. Now, I nodded.
"It would explain why he doesn't remember anything," I
said, bending my head close to Eve's and keeping my
voice down.

"And you think somebody might have used one of
those date rape drugs?"

This wasn't the time to discuss the theory, so I simply
nodded. Luckily, not much had happened to Noel in high
school. He quickly finished and sat down. That's when
Celia walked up to the podium and I perked up. No one

knew a woman like her friends did, and I hoped to learn a lot about Vickie from what Celia had to say.

"Last Thursday," Celia began, but her voice clogged and she turned her head and cleared her throat. "Last Thursday, when I went to my son's school for parent-teacher conferences, I can't tell you how many people stopped me in the hallways to talk about Vickie. People remember her as a perfect and tireless volunteer and a terrific organizer. If you needed someone to chair the annual harvest festival party for the kids, Vickie was your man. Er . . . your woman," Celia added, and a reverent murmur of laughter filled the room.

"Vickie was at every single one of Henry's soccer games." She looked at the little boy who was, by this time, sitting on his father's lap. "She always brought homemade snacks for all the kids on the team—both teams. She always wrote thank-you notes to the coaches at the end of the season. She was the first to raise her hand when Antonia's Girl Scout troop needed a cookie mom or a car pool coordinator. Every single person in this room is going to miss Vickie. But it's important to remember that we aren't the only ones who will feel this loss. McLean will not be as good a place without Vickie among us."

Celia sat down and Glynis took her place. "Vickie was absolutely the most wonderful woman in the whole world." She giggled a little in that uncomfortable way people do when they're not sure if they should be laughing or not. "If you knew her, this isn't news to you. You know she was beautiful, and that she took pride in her looks. You know she kept a perfect house, and that if the Big Guy up there"—Glynis looked toward the ceiling— "if the Big Guy ever decides to re-create the Garden of Eden, he'll ask for Vickie's advice. She was gifted when it came to gardening and decorating, and she could throw one heck of a party. There isn't one . . ." Glynis turned toward the urn on the table. "There isn't one party any of us will ever have or ever attend that we won't think of you, sweetie. We'll miss you."

Beth was waiting at the podium even before Glynis walked away. "Vickie loved her family," she said. "Edward . . ." Beth's eyes welled and her voice wobbled over the words. "She loved you, Edward, and you know she was the perfect wife. She loved you, Antonia. And you, Henry. Your mommy is looking down on you right now from heaven. She'll always . . . always . . ." It was all Beth could say. Sobbing, she returned to her seat.

Sobbing, we all watched her.

After that, things wrapped up pretty quickly. On behalf of the family, the funeral director thanked everyone for coming and invited friends and relatives to the Monroe home for lunch. We all stood and, row by row, filed past the urn.

Because Eve and I were in the back row, we were the first out the door. But when she made to go out to the parking lot, I put a hand on her arm. "I want to talk to them," I said. "To Vickie's friends."

Eve was taller than me. She didn't even have to strain to look over my head and back into the room where the service had been conducted. I looked that way, too, and saw Celia, Glynis, and Beth, their arms linked, standing in front of the urn. "What are you going to say? That you're trying to find their friend's killer? They know Alex is in custody."

"I was thinking I'd say I was a friend from college, that I heard about Vickie and—"

Just as I was practicing the lie, the three women walked out of the room. They stood in a tight circle, their arms around each other, and well-prepared lie or not, I didn't have the heart to butt in.

But then, I didn't have the luxury of not butting in, either. Not if I intended to get to the bottom of Vickie's murder.

Just as I approached, Glynis pulled out of the hug. "We should go Wednesday after school," she said to her friends, sniffing. "We always go on Wednesdays, and the kids will be disappointed if we don't. We don't want to upset them. We don't want to let them know how upset we are. Besides, we owe it to ourselves to keep things as normal as we possibly can."

"You're right." Celia nodded.

Beth said, "I promised Erin we'd do Clemyjontri Park this week."

"That's fine," said Celia.

"Agreed," said Glynis. "Four o'clock?"

And when nobody objected, the three women split up and went to stand with their husbands.

Watching them go, Eve leaned over my shoulder. "You're not going to tell them you're an old friend from college?"

"I've got a better idea." No one was paying any attention to me, but I turned away anyway when the three friends walked toward the door. "I'm not going to be an old friend, I'm going to be a new friend," I told Eve. And before she could ask for details I hadn't thought of yet, we turned and left the funeral home.

WHEN IT COMES TO PLAYGROUNDS, CLEMYJONTRI Park is something of a legend. At least in this part of Virginia. It features four different play areas with a carousel in the center, and though I'd read that the play-

ground took up the better part of two acres, that didn't
quite translate. At least not until I arrived there Wednesday at four and realized it wasn't going to be easy to find
Celia, Glynis, and Beth. I trudged over just about the
entire playground before I caught sight of them watching
a horde of children scramble over the jungle gym in the
Fun and Fitness area.

That was just about the time I realized something
else—showing up at a playground without a kid made
me stick out like a sore thumb.

If I was as thorough and as organized as I claimed to
be, why didn't I think of that?

I swallowed my mortification and thanked my lucky
stars that Eve wasn't able to be with me that day. One
woman without children was odd. Two were bound to
look conspicuous. As it turned out, Eve said she had too
much to do that afternoon. She claimed she was going
to zip over to Très Bonne Cuisine so she and Norman
could look through samples to choose the napkins that
would be on the table at the wedding. (Just for the record, I insisted that the napkins Bellywasher's already
owned would be fine, but once Eve and Norman got the
whole cotton sateen idea in their heads, they were impossible to control.) No matter, I didn't believe the table
linen story from the start. Oh, no. My worries ran far
deeper. I had suspicions about another wedding cake
fiasco. Believe me, as soon as I had a free minute to de-
vote to it, I was going to go into full detective mode and
call every bakery in Arlington and beyond. One sparkler-
encrusted wedding cake per lifetime is one too many.

I promised myself I'd think about that another time.
For now, I had a murder to investigate. With that in mind,
I walked over to the Fun and Fitness area like I had every

right to be there. When I stopped to look things over, I just so happened to end up close to where Celia, Glynis, and Beth were talking quietly.

"Wow." When I pulled in a breath of wonder, I didn't have to fake it. The place was spectacular. Besides, I was out of breath from walking the playground. "I've heard good things about this place, but I never thought it would be so incredible. The kids are going to love this!"

Celia turned and offered me a smile. "You didn't bring your kids? When they find out, they're going to declare you Monster Mommy."

We all laughed. I took that as a good sign and moved a casual step closer. "They've got music lessons this afternoon. All three of them," I said, lying through my teeth—about the music lessons and, of course, about the three kids—and not caring a bit since it was all for a good cause. "I figured it was a good time to come check things out."

"You're new to the area?" The question came from Glynis, and since it played into the persona I'd made up for myself on the drive to Fairfax County, I was all set to jump right in.

"Just moved in," I said. "We bought a house in the Humboldt Creek development."

"That's where we all live!" Have no fear, I didn't tremble when Glynis made the announcement. I had the tasteful program the funeral chapel gave out at Vickie's service, remember, so I knew all these women's last names. I'd looked up their addresses, and I'd even cruised by their homes a couple times. I knew there were two new streets being added to the upscale elegance of Humboldt Creek. I saw that on those streets, a few of the houses were finished and people were already moving in. In my mind, I'd decided which of those houses I was going to pretend was mine. It was a redbrick Colonial with white shutters and a brick front walk. I'd just seen the moving truck out front on Tuesday, and when I drove by that Wednesday afternoon, there were already pots of tulips outside the front door and off-white draperies, tasteful and simple, hanging in the windows. There was a Lexus in the driveway, a landscaper busily at work manicuring the lawn, and a couple kids' bikes leaning against the garage door.

Hey, I can dream, can't I?

"What a coincidence." I pretended it was and offered Celia and Glynis a smile in turn. When I got to Beth, I had to wait. She was distracted yelling to her son, Jeremy, who looked to be about eight, that he should take it easy because he had practice with the Tigers later that evening and he was going to tire himself out. That taken care of, she wrinkled her nose and gave me a careful look.

"You were at Vickie's funeral," Beth said.

At the funeral, they'd been so preoccupied with their own grief, I hadn't expected any of them to notice me, and I silently cursed myself. Out loud I said, "Oh, my gosh, wasn't it just awful? I never knew Vickie, of course. I mean, we just moved here from Chicago so I don't know anyone in the area at all yet. But I read about her murder in the paper and I saw that she lived nearby and I just had to pay my respects. As a neighbor. And a mom."

Tears streamed down Beth's cheeks. I didn't have to lie when I said, "I'm so sorry. Now I recognize you. All of you." Celia sniffed and fished a tissue out of her pocket. Glynis's bottom lip trembled. "You were her friends. I remember seeing you in the front row at the funeral chapel. I'm so very sorry. I didn't mean to bring up bad memories."

"Oh, there aren't any bad memories. Not where Vickie is concerned." Beth laughed through her tears. "She was so wonderful. I'm just glad they found the creep who did that to her."

"But why?" When all three women looked at me in wonder, I knew I had to explain myself. "Not why are you glad they found him," I said, pretending to be embarrassed by the gaffe. "Why did he do it? It's just so awful to think about. I can't imagine anyone would stab a woman to death. Not unless they were involved or something and it was a sort of lovers' quarrel."

"No way." Glynis slashed one hand through the air. "Did you see something like that in the papers? Because I'll tell you right now, no way that's true."

"Then she didn't know him?" I asked.

"I can't even imagine she knew where that bar was." This came from Beth. She paused and glanced at her friends. "Well, can any of you? Vickie was such a home-body. She would never hang around in a bar by herself."

"Only she wasn't by herself," I reminded them.

"Vickie wasn't the type who snuck around and did things behind her husband's back," Celia added. "She never would have been in that bar alone. And she sure never would have been carrying on with somebody. It's crazy."

"But the cops think that guy . . . I think I read his name was Alex . . . they say that this Alex guy did it. Do you have any theories about why he would?"

Celia shook her head. Glynis stared at the ground. Beth started crying all over again.

And I knew I wasn't going to get another thing out of them. "Look, I really am sorry to have dredged up so much sorrow," I said, relieved that at least I could be honest about this. "I'm sorry you lost your friend in such a horrible way, and I'm truly sorry because I can see that you're going to miss her terribly."

"She was perfect," Celia said, and it struck me that it wasn't the first time I'd heard the word. I remembered the eulogies these women had given back at the funeral. Each one of them had used that word, *perfect*.

Perfect friend.

Perfect wife.

Perfect mother.

Vickie Monroe was perfect.

So what was she doing hanging out in a bar every Tuesday night?

And if she was so perfect, why would anybody want to kill her?

Five

◼

APPARENTLY THE COPS HAD ALREADY BROKEN THE news to Alex. That would explain why when he walked into the visitors' room at the jail that Wednesday evening, the first thing out of his mouth was, "I didn't know, Annie. Honest, I didn't know that Vickie was married."

If Alex was a liar, he was a mighty good one. When he sat down in the chair across from mine, I studied the pained expression on his face.

"They think it's why I killed her," he said on the end of a sigh. "They think that maybe I didn't know, and that Vickie, she told me that night that she was married and that I wasn't happy hearing it." His voice faded; his gaze was suddenly unfocused. It took him a couple seconds to come out of his funk, but when he did, his eyes snapped right to mine. "I never knew until the police told me. I swear to God."

"And I believe you." The guard outside the door happened to be watching, or I would have reached across the table to give Alex's hand a squeeze.

"Jim couldn't come." Since I was alone, it was an obvious thing for him to say, but I forgave him. In a place like this—in a situation this insane—it was only natural for Alex to think about his friend and cousin.

"You know how the restaurant business can be. There was some problem with a beer delivery today and Damien, one of our cooks, has been sick. Jim wanted to be here—"

"But he's busy. Aye. I understand. And I know he'll come by when he has a chance." Alex shifted in his chair. "And the house? I feel so awful about the house, Annie. The redecorating, it's my gift to you and Jim. And now . . ."

"It doesn't matter." It didn't. But a thing not mattering and that same thing not being of burning interest, those are two different things. I tried not to sound too eager when I said, "I'm sure you've already accomplished a whole lot in the house. You probably got the living and the dining room done, and . . ." I drew out the last word, encouraging him to chime right in.

Instead, Alex laughed. I shouldn't have been offended, seeing as how I'd intended to cheer him up with this visit. I wouldn't have been offended if he didn't shake his head in wonder. "You're brazen, you know that, woman? Even here in a jail in the midst of the worst thing that's ever happened to me—"

"I'm sorry," I groaned. "I can't help myself."

"And I don't hold it against ye. And I do appreciate all you're doing for me. There couldn't be any better friends in the world than you and Jim. I owe you for that, surely."

Hope blossomed in my heart. It had nothing to do

with my case, and everything to do with finding out what was happening inside the home I would soon be living in. I sat up. Smiled. Leaned forward, eager to hear more.

Alex sat back and crossed his arms over his chest. "I'm not sayin' another word. Not about the house."

"But . . . but . . ." I was stammering and it wasn't pretty. Then again, Alex was a relative (or soon would be) and I didn't have to put on a front for him. I stammered some more. "You said . . . what about appreciating what I'm doing for you? And . . . and . . . visiting here . . . and—"

He interrupted me with a laugh. "Wish I could help. Can't. I'm sworn to secrecy by Jim. And in case you haven't heard it lately, Jim and I—"

"Like brothers. Yeah, I know." I, too, sank back in my chair. "I could blackmail you, tell you that if you don't let the cat out of the redecorating bag, I won't work on your case."

"And I could promise all the broken biscuit cake you like, as soon as I'm out of this place."

Talk about a stalemate.

I swallowed my pride and opted for the cake. "All right," I said. "But this isn't about gluttony, it's about respecting Jim's wishes."

"Which means you're still my personal private eye?"

"I wish I had better news." I went through what I knew about the case so far. It didn't take long. I waited until the end to bring up the two things that were bothering me most. "What are the chances you were drugged?" I asked Alex.

Thinking, he cocked his head. "I can say this much for sure: I had only a couple of glasses of beer, so that surely shouldn't have knocked me on my arse. And if I was drunk, it was a drunk like I've never felt before.

When I woke up in that alley . . ." A shiver skittered across his broad shoulders. He twitched the memory aside and started again. "My head was poundin', my heart was racin'. I thought it was all due to being arrested. You know, you don't expect to open your eyes and the very first thing you see is a police officer with his gun trained on you and the second thing you see is a body, a woman, dead." He looked away. "Yes, I could have been drugged, I suppose. But wouldn't I have noticed something?"

"How about someone?" I'd been itching to ask. "If someone slipped something in your beer, that same someone must have been hanging around your table."

Frustrated, he shook his head. "We were dancing. And it was crowded. Even then, you think when I came back to the table and took a drink—"

"If everything I've read on the Internet is true, date rape drugs are pretty much colorless and odorless. Some of them have a slightly salty taste, but you were drinking dark, heavy beer. You probably wouldn't even notice."

"And a drug like that, would it explain why I don't remember?"

"It might. It might also explain why you passed out, and why when you did, the killer was able to put that knife in your hands."

"But there's no way to prove it?"

I knew my expression gave Alex all the answer he needed.

Since he was already in a bad mood, I didn't feel guilty bringing up my visit to Swallows. "The girl who waited on you—"

"Jennifer."

"That's right. I don't know if the police have spoken to her yet, but I'll bet they have. And I bet she told them what she told me. Alex, according to Jennifer, you threatened Vickie. You said you wished she was dead."

He winced as if I'd slapped him. "Dead?" The way he said it, it sounded like *daid*. He scraped a hand through his mane of red hair. "Are you daft, Annie? I'd never in my life say that to a woman, certainly not to one I was trying to impress. Give me some credit, I know the way to a woman's heart isn't through threatening her."

If he was right, someone was lying.

And I was left with more questions than I'd come into the jail with.

IF I WAS GOING TO FIND OUT WHAT REALLY happened in that alley outside of Swallows and how Alex was involved, I had to get closer to Vickie's life. I mean, closer than just claiming I'd moved into that fabulous Colonial with the brick walk.

This, of course, would have been easier to do if real life didn't keep intruding.

Not that I'm complaining. When *real life* means my wedding . . .

I stepped back. Or at least I tried to. In the minuscule dressing room of that big-ticket boutique near Swallows, there wasn't a lot of room to move. Still, I managed to give Eve a careful look.

She was standing in the center of the tiny dais in front of the full-length mirror, looking like a million bucks in that green cocktail dress with skinny straps and the neckline that was cut low enough to reveal not only some cleavage but, I swear, some of her abdomen, too.

"I don't know," I said, and because I knew the instant Eve's golden eyebrows dipped that she was about to take the comment the wrong way, I jumped right in with an apology. "It's not that you don't look terrific. You do. You really do. It's just that the dress . . ." I gave Eve and the garment in question another look. The dress still had the price tag attached and though I'd promised myself the first time I saw it and gagged that I would not look again, I couldn't help myself. "It's awfully expensive. And it's awfully formal. When I told you to pick any dress you wanted—"

Eve wrinkled her nose. "You didn't mean it?"

There it was again, that little look, and the tiny catch in Eve's voice that betrayed the fact that I'd hurt her feelings. Like I had any other choice but to apologize again?

"Of course I meant it," I said. It was true, even though looking back on the day I'd announced that Jim and I were not going to have a formal wedding and that any dress Eve picked to wear would work just fine . . . well, I guess I should have known then that my offer was going to be taken the wrong way. And that it was going to get me in trouble, to boot.

"My dress is simplicity itself," I reminded her even though she should have known it since Eve was with me when I picked out the dress. "Sleeveless satin sheath. Little bolero with a bead-trimmed collar. It's not that I don't love the dress you're wearing. I really do, Eve. It's just that—"

"I get it. Sackcloth and ashes." I would have been offended—or at least embarrassed—if Eve didn't laugh.

Instead, I rolled my eyes. "You'd make even sackcloth and ashes look good," I told her, and by the way she smiled, I'm pretty sure she knew it was true.

"So . . ." She carefully took off the green dress and even though she wasn't considering it for the wedding, she'd brought another dress into the room with her. It was a cute (and very short) little silk sleeveless number with a gathered waist, tie-dyed in every shade of blue in the crayon box. The dress was too casual, even for my wedding, but in Eve's book, that didn't mean she couldn't try it on.

She slipped her head through the V-necked opening. "Are you really going to try and find out what made Vickie tick? I mean, by hanging around with her friends?"

We'd talked about the plan on the way over to the boutique, but since Eve was driving at the time and since driving and Eve are almost as impossible a combination as Eve and not trying on beautiful clothes when they're within an arm's length, I knew she hadn't been paying a whole lot of attention.

"It's the perfect plan," I reminded her. "And as far as I can see, it's the only way to try and make some sense of this whole thing. What would make a perfect wife and mother hang out regularly in a bar with a man she had no intention of ever having any sort of real relationship with? I don't know, Eve, I just don't get it."

Eve turned this way and that, the better to see herself from all sides in the mirror. Every side looked good. "Maybe Vickie was lonely," she said. "Or maybe she hated her life."

"What was to hate? She had a successful husband, two beautiful little kids, a fabulous home. I should know, I've driven by the house a couple times, just to try and get a sense of what kind of woman she was. And I've learned a lot. The house is showy. I mean, three stories, a circular drive, landscaped to the nth degree. So I know she liked things to be just so. And I know she and Edward must have a healthy income, because there's no way anybody lives in a house like that unless they've got money to burn. What I don't know is anything about Vickie personally. If I can get in good with Celia, Glynis, and Beth . . . well, they were her best friends. They knew her better than anybody did."

"So you're going to pretend you live in the neighborhood? That you're one of them?"

The way Eve said it, it would be like admitting I was an alien being beamed down from a faraway planet. "Is it that weird? They're women. I'm a woman. They're wives. I'm almost a wife. And I used to be a wife, remember. They're mothers and, no, I'm not. But that doesn't mean I haven't been paying attention all these years. Lots of mothers come into Bellywasher's. I hear them talking about their kids. And lots of them used to come into the bank with their kids." Some of the memories of those incidents made me cringe. "I've seen it all, Eve. I can talk the talk and I can walk the walk."

"And you're not just doing this to try and satisfy some fantasy you have about your dream life as a suburban wife and mother?"

When it comes to psychology, Eve is not usually so insightful. In fact, she's not usually insightful at all. The fact that this was a momentous occasion showed just how close we were as friends. She could practically read my mind.

All the more reason I had to deny it.

"Really, Eve, you know I'm not that type."

She gave herself another once-over in the mirror, then checked out the price tag on the dress again. "And what type is that?" she asked. "The type who isn't afraid to admit that even though she's practical and down-to-earth, it doesn't hurt to dream once in a while? You know, go crazy and go after the wild impossibilities."

"You mean like you wearing that green cocktail dress to my wedding."

"I mean, there's nothing wrong with saying you want a big house and a great, successful husband, and a whole bunch of wonderful, beautiful kids."

"I am going to have a great husband," I reminded her. "The greatest. And yes, I'd like a whole bunch of wonderful, beautiful kids. One of these days. As far as the successful husband, I'm willing to judge success any way Jim does. If that means Bellywasher's turns a profit at the end of the year, that's good enough for me. If it means some rah-rah write-up in one of the local papers, that's OK, too. As far as the big house, I know better than that. I'm not kidding myself. And I'm not jealous of people who do have incredible houses. I'm happy with what I have."

"That's why you're going to pretend you're one of them."

"It's not like I'm trying to scam them out of their life savings or anything." This went without saying, but I said it anyway. "All I'm trying to do is get close. To get information."

Another look at the dress, and Eve made up her mind. I wasn't sure if that meant *buy* or *don't buy*, so I waited patiently to find out while she got dressed again. "You know you've got a couple problems," she said as we walked out of the dressing room and back through the store. "When you ran into those women at the playground, you told me that you told them that you had kids."

"And I do."

When she looked at me in wonder, I had to laugh. The explanation was easy enough. "Fiona."

"Oh, Jim's cousin!" Eve's eyes lit up. "Fiona has eight

kids. I get it. You're going to send Fiona to McLean to pretend she's you."

I bit my tongue. At least until I was sure I could speak without being too critical. "I stopped in and talked to Fiona this morning. She was frazzled. As usual. And who can blame her? Just the prospect of getting three of the kids out of her hair for a couple hours made her light up like a Christmas tree."

When Eve is thinking very hard, her forehead furrows. If she knew it, she'd be appalled. That might explain why she tries never to think very hard. She set the tie-dyed dress on the counter, opened her purse, and pulled out her American Express. "So three of Fiona's kids are going to go to McLean and they're going to . . ." It was too much. She gave up with a shrug. "I don't see how they're going to find out anything about Vickie. Those friends of hers, they're not going to talk about their murdered buddy with kids."

About this time, my tongue was corrugated. I waited until Eve paid and the pleasant clerk packed the dress up in a shiny black shopping bag with the name of the boutique emblazoned on the side.

"I'm not going to send the girls in my place," I said, leading the way out of the store. "They're going to come with me."

"Because . . ." Inspiration hit, and Eve's blue eyes gleamed. "You're going to pretend they're your daughters!"

Now that we were on the same page, it was far easier to explain. "Lucy, Emma, and Doris have dance class after school on Thursdays, so I can't take them. It's probably just as well. They're the oldest and it would be harder to pull the wool over someone's eyes with three girls along who know enough about honesty—and dishonesty—to have the scruples to spill the beans." We stepped out onto the sidewalk and headed toward where Eve had parked her car.

"I'm going to take Gloria, Wendy, and Rosemary, instead. They're close enough in age to keep each other busy while I do what I have to do, and young enough—I hope—to believe me when I tell them I'm playing a kind of joke on some people and need them to pretend I'm their mom."

Little did I know just how prophetic that statement would turn out to be. Later that afternoon, no sooner had I pulled out of Fi and Richard's driveway than the girls started acting exactly like they do when their mother is in charge. In other words, they teased, punched, had a screaming contest, and generally carried on all the way to McLean.

By the time we got to the soccer fields behind the Spring Hill Recreation Center, I was grateful that I had my case to think about. I'd do it, too, as soon as my brain settled down and my ears stopped ringing. With that in mind, I told the girls they could go over to the nearby play area and turned my attention to the crowd of moms and dads watching the Tigers out on the field. Celia, Glynis, and Beth were there, just as I expected them to be, and I put on my game face (the one I hoped would make it look like I was surprised to run into them again) and headed in their direction.

Am I psychic? *Au contraire*, as our friend the former Jacques Lavoie would say. In fact, it wasn't extrasensory powers or good luck I had to thank for this encounter. It was good ol' detective work, computers, and a little psychology. See, I may not know the difference between a saucepot and a frying pan, but I'm pretty savvy when it comes to Googling my way around the Internet. That's where I found the Tigers soccer schedule. And the psychology? Well, my ex, Peter, is a high school chemistry teacher, and back when we were together, we spent a lot of time with other teachers and their families. Being the only one at the time without at least one small child, I didn't exactly fit in, but when the mothers talked, I listened. And learned. One of the things I learned is that friends often get their children involved in the same activities. If Beth's Jeremy played for the Tigers, my money was on Celia's and Glynis's kids playing on the team, too.

Oh, how I love it when I'm right!

"Celia!" I caught her eye first and closed in. "And Beth and Glynis. What a surprise!"

"Your kids play?" Celia was dressed in blue and white, the colors of the Tigers uniforms. She beamed a smile at me and leaned nearer. "Not on the Rangers, I hope. I hear their coach is a real bear."

"Oh, no. No soccer for us. The girls just needed to blow off some steam." I looked over at the play area and at the exact right moment, Wendy waved. I couldn't have asked for better proof that I was there with real, honest-to-goodness kids. "I didn't realize there was a soccer game going on."

"Over on the right, Eli!" Before she turned to me, Glynis yelled to a little boy who looked exactly like her, down to the ash-gray eyes. She, too, was dressed in team colors: blue workout pants, a matching jacket, and a white T-shirt. "Well, this is terrific. We were wondering if we'd see you again. We thought maybe we'd run into you at Churchill Road School."

Not to worry. Like I said, I'd done my homework. If I found out these women's children went to private school, I was all set to say mine attended public. If they said public, I'd say exactly what I said, "We're at St. John's."

"Good school." Beth, looking like the ultimate fan in a blue jumper and white blouse, with a huge Tigers button pinned to her chest, never took her eyes off the game. Jeremy was in the center of the field, standing as still as a statue and looking bewildered while the other boys raced around him and toward the goal. "Go, Jeremy!" Beth yelled, and when the little boy didn't, she didn't care, she just yelled some more.

Good friend or not, Celia rolled her eyes. Of course, since Beth was watching the game, she didn't see it. That gave Glynis a chance to elbow Celia in the ribs.

I pretended not to notice any of it. Instead, I looked over at the play area to make sure the girls weren't causing any trouble. When I looked back at the game, I realized Celia was looking at the play area, too.

"They don't look a thing like you," she said.

"The girls?" Of course she was talking about the girls. Who else would she be talking about? I laughed. "They've got my curly hair." They did, but that had to do with chance, not genetics. "Everything else they got from their father."

"He's a redhead?" For one terrible moment, I thought Glynis had made some unlikely and mistaken connection between me and Alex. He, after all, had the flaming hair that cousin Fi inherited from the Bannerman side of the family and her children had gotten from her. If these women thought I had anything to do with the man who'd been charged with killing their friend . . .

I swallowed down the worry. Alex wasn't the only red-haired man in the world. "It's their Scottish ancestors," I said, as truthful as can be. "They got the whole package: the red hair, the freckles, even the tempers. From my family—" A man over on our right attracted my attention, and I didn't have to worry about bringing my family into this. I was so startled, I blurted out, "Is that Edward Monroe? He's the soccer coach?"

"The best in the league." Glynis slid me a look. "At least he's always been the best in the league. Today, I'm not so sure."

"Well, the fact that his wife just died might have something to do with it." I shouldn't have had to point this out. "Isn't it a little weird that he'd be here coaching? I mean, after what happened?"

Celia shook her head. There was a folding table of refreshments set up nearby and maybe it was almost halftime or intermission or whatever it is they have in soccer games. She went over to the table, and because it looked like she might talk if I encouraged her a bit, I followed. When she opened a giant bottle of Gatorade, I held out paper cups for her to fill—just like any seasoned mom would have done at a child's sports event.

Celia was neat and efficient. When she finished with one bottle of Gatorade, she opened another. "Like Glyn said, Edward is the best in the league. He'd never let the boys down and not show up for a game. Even if it means setting his own grief aside for a while. Henry's on the team . . ." Celia looked over at the boys and I did, too, and spotted Vickie's son. "It's good for Henry to be with his friends. He needs the break, too."

"Of course." Celia ran out of paper cups and since there was a new bag of them nearby, I opened it, slipped more cups from the plastic sleeve, and got back to work. We were far enough away that Glynis and Beth couldn't hear us, so I took a chance at being nosy. "What did Glynis mean, about Edward usually being the best coach in the league except for today? Is there a problem?"

"In case you haven't noticed, the problem is Jeremy." On cue, the ball careened Jeremy's way and he reacted instinctively. He caught it in his hands. Jim is a fan of what he calls *football* and those of us in the United States call *soccer*. Me? Not so much. But I guess I've sat beside him as he watched enough games on TV that some of the rules and regulations have seeped into my brain through osmosis. Even I know that, except for the goalkeeper, none of the players is allowed to touch the ball. Celia knew it, too, of course. She cringed. "I love the kid to pieces. Honest. But when it comes to soccer, he's hopeless. He's so bad, Edward doesn't even usually let him play."

"And today he did?"

Finished with the Gatorade, she shrugged and reached for a box of donut holes. She arranged them by flavor on paper plates, each little round donut precisely set against the other so that by the time she was done, the arrangements looked like stylized flowers. "Maybe Edward's just feeling soft and sappy. You know, because of the funeral and all. I hope it doesn't last. My Carter is a talented athlete. I'd hate to see his college scholarship chances dwindle because he's on a losing team."

I laughed, and when I saw Celia's lips thin, I knew instantly that I shouldn't have. "I just didn't think . . ." It was scramble to apologize or look like a complete fool. "I don't think I'd be worried about college right now. These kids are in, what, first grade?"

Celia's smile was stiff. "Carter is in kindergarten. But it's never too soon to think about college. Not if you expect your kids to get into a good school. Your girls, what kinds of activities are they involved in?"

"Dance class for one. And music." It was the only thing I could think of. "We're waiting to be a little more settled before we get involved in too much else."

"There's a great girls' team." Apparently, it was break

time. The boys streamed off the field, and as they did, Celia handed each a paper cup. Glynis came to help. Though from my experience I would have said little boys didn't need to be directed toward donut holes or any other sweets, she gestured toward the plates and told the boys they were each allowed two.

Beth, I noted, waited for Jeremy to walk off the field and when he did, she brought him over, her arm around his shoulders.

"Didn't he do great?" she asked no one in particular.

"I did not." Jeremy scuffed the toe of his shoe on the ground. "I stink."

"You need practice. Everyone needs practice," Celia assured him.

"Everyone has their own special gifts," Glynis added. "You're a good artist, Jeremy. I've seen the pictures you draw. You can't expect to be good at everything."

Jeremy's bottom lip protruded. "Carter is," he grumbled.

"It's true," Celia whispered to me, and said to Jeremy, "But you're not Carter. And you can't measure yourself based on what Carter does. You can only be the best Jeremy you can possibly be." I doubt the kid noticed the sour expression that pinched her face. "If you are, then maybe Coach will let you play in another game."

"As a matter of fact, Edward already said Jeremy could play the second half," Beth announced and, jazzed by the news, Jeremy grabbed four donut holes and headed for the spot where the rest of his team was gathered. Parental pride gleaming from her eyes, Beth watched him. "Edward says Jeremy is going to play in every game for the rest of the season. Isn't that wonderful news?"

Before anyone could come up with an answer that was

truthful or hurtful, I figured it was the perfect time to change the subject. "So . . ." I had questions I wanted to ask, plenty of them. The trick, as always, was figuring out how to get information without looking too obvious. "Any more news about Vickie's murder?" I asked.

OK, it may have been obvious, but honestly, if I didn't ask, that would have been obvious, too.

For a couple moments, I thought nobody heard me. Celia kept busy rearranging the donut holes. She consolidated them so there were two flavors per plate. With a practiced eye, Glynis looked around the area to make sure there were no paper cups thrown on the ground. That left Beth, and I knew she heard me because at the mention of Vickie's name, she got as pale as the white blouse she was wearing with her jumper.

"There's nothing else to know," Beth said, her voice suddenly breathy. "The police say they have the killer. Once he's tried and convicted, we'll all get the closure we need."

Not all of us.

I, of course, did not point this out.

Instead, I snapped up a donut hole. Glazed. No, I hadn't been offered one, but just as Eve couldn't be close to beautiful clothing and not go into covet mode I couldn't be within sight of sweets and not go for it. Fortunately, these ladies didn't hold it against me.

"What I don't get"—I popped the donut hole in my mouth—"is why Vickie was hanging out with the guy they say killed her in the first place. And at that bar so far from home. Did you know she went there every Tuesday?"

"Every Tuesday?" Glynis's face took on a color that matched her eyes. "That's impossible. How do you—"

"Read it in the newspaper. Don't ask me which one;

we get a few different papers at home. But I know one of them mentioned that the guy they arrested . . . Alex somebody, I think the newspaper said . . . and one of them said that he told the cops that he and Vickie met at the restaurant every Tuesday."

"Look, they're about to get started again!" Jeremy was back on the field, and I might as well have been invisible. Beth completely ignored me and zoomed right by. She went to stand at the edge of the field, cheering for Jeremy with all her might.

Celia rolled her eyes.

"Something tells me that look has nothing to do with Vickie and everything to do with soccer," I said.

"You got that right." When Jeremy never moved a muscle and a kid from the other team kicked the ball away from him, she sighed. "Here we go again."

"So Vickie never said anything to you? I mean, about going out with this Alex guy every Tuesday night?"

If Celia was surprised that I was so single-minded, she didn't show it. Carter did something she considered spectacular and she applauded. "The only things Vickie ever talked to us about were friend things. You know, school and parties, our houses and our husbands."

I dared to push it, just a little. "Friends talk about lovers, too."

"But he wasn't a lover," Glynis said. She sounded like she knew what she was talking about, which to me meant that Vickie had told these women about Alex. Otherwise, how would they know he was not a lover? "Vickie wasn't the type to step out. In fact, the only place she ever went was the only place all of us ever go. Cooking class."

Good thing I'd already swallowed my donut hole, or I might have choked. Talk of cooking does that to me.

I pasted a smile on my face. "Cooking classes? I've taken cooking classes, over at Très Bonne Cuisine in Arlington."

"We go to Sonny's in Reston." Glynis sounded as if this was something to be proud of and for all I know, it may have been. It's hard to think past the brain freeze that always gets to me when the subject of cooking comes up. She smiled at Celia.

"Annie knows how to cook," she told Celia. "She's taken cooking classes."

Celia grinned. "Are you thinking what I'm thinking?" she asked her friend, and apparently, Glynis was.

Celia closed in on me. "The next wine tasting is at Beth's house Friday," she said. "I know what you're going to say. Isn't it a little soon after Vickie's passing? But really, Annie, you didn't know her. She would have wanted it this way. Beth won't mind you joining us. You'll come?"

It was exactly the kind of in I was hoping for. I nodded my consent.

"Good." Celia gave me the address. "This week we're tasting zinfandels, so bring a bottle and an appetizer and your husband, too, of course."

"If you could come a little early . . ." Glynis leaned in.

"Five?" Celia asked the question, but didn't wait for an answer before she added, "Beth's helping out at school that day, but she should be back in time. If not, no worries. We all know where each other's hide-a-keys are, so someone will be there to let you in. We're officially making you our designated cooking expert."

The Tigers scored and it was a good thing they did. Otherwise they would have heard me squeak, "Designated? Expert?" When the crowd finally settled, I told them I was looking forward to the wine tasting.

After all, what else could I do?

I sure couldn't tell them the truth.

In my experience, the only thing cooking classes led to was culinary disasters.

Oh, yeah, and murder.

Six

⌗

"ME? DESIGNATED COOKING EXPERT? YOU CAN SEE why this is a bad thing, right? I mean, what if they actually ask my advice about cooking? Or . . ."

Yes, I'd been obsessing, practically since the moment Celia, Glynis, and Beth invited me to join them at their next wine tasting. But I'd been stuck on the whole meaning of what, exactly, a designated cooking expert was. Now I had a whole new worry and, thinking about it, panic filled me like ice water. My hand was already on Jim's arm, and it tightened like a blood pressure cuff.

"What if they actually expect me to cook?" I squeaked.

He laughed. But then, Jim is a predictable kind of guy. It's one of the reasons I love him. Except when it comes to talk of cooking, of course.

One by one, he pried my fingers from his sleeve and shook his arm. I think he was trying to get the circulation back. "Have I taught you nothing?" he asked. "When it comes to cooking, you can hold your own."

"I can't. You're just saying that because—"

"Because it's true."

"Because you love me and you're trying to make me feel better."

"I love you." He gave me a quick kiss. "I'm trying to make you feel better." Another kiss, a little longer and a little slower, and I was actually beginning to believe him. "You can hold your own when it comes to cooking. With anyone."

Even another kiss wasn't enough to make me believe that. It was Thursday evening, and Bellywasher's had just closed. The only ones left in the restaurant were Larry, Hank, and Charlie, three of our usuals, who'd stopped in late after their bowling league and ordered the day's blue plate special: hot dogs, beans, and fries. (Just for the record, the blue plate special is never on the menu. No one besides Larry, Hank, and Charlie even knows about it. Jim keeps a supply of hot dogs just for them because they've been coming to Bellywasher's for, like, forever. See? Didn't I say that Jim was the greatest guy in the world?)

We were standing in the kitchen, and I pushed away from Jim, the better to wring my hands and pace. "They take classes, Jim. Over at Sonny's. I've heard you talk about Sonny's. It's a good cooking school."

"Sonny Fleming has a reputation, that's sure enough. He's got good technique. He's excellent when it comes to presentation. I hear his shop isn't nearly as well stocked as Jacques' . . . er, Norman's . . ." Force of habit. Jim twitched away the slip of the tongue and continued. "Sonny's gaining a reputation. He's a fine, skilled chef and a marketing genius, as well. He's making a name for himself."

"And these ladies are actually interested enough to

take lessons from him. Go figure." I couldn't, because I'd never wanted to take that first cooking class back when Eve signed us up for it. She was trying to cheer me up after my divorce, and in the great scheme of things, I guess it worked. That class was where I met Jim, and got my first introduction to murder and to being a detective.

Even that wasn't enough to lift my spirits.

I thought of the stove that had once exploded right in my face at Très Bonne Cuisine. "What if they ask me to bake bread?"

"It takes hours to make bread. There's no time for that at a wine tasting."

I remembered all the foods I'd taken to new heights of crispness. "Then what if they want me to cook the main course or something? What if it's a rack of lamb? Or fondue? Oh, my gosh, do you remember right after we first started dating and you came over for dinner and I was trying to impress you so I made dessert fondue?"

No doubt Jim did. But then, it's hard to forget an evening where we spent hours getting the chocolate splatters off the countertops, the cupboards, and the kitchen floor. Even that, though, wasn't enough to deter him. "A wine tasting means cheese and nibblers. Nothing more. And you know a thing or two about cheese, don't you?"

"I know that when I don't burn it, Velveeta melts well."

Jim rolled his eyes. "You dinna learn that from me, that's sure enough. Concentrate, Annie, and think of all you've picked up here at Bellywasher's. Try again. Tell me what you know about Asiago."

I took a deep breath and closed my eyes. "Fresh Asiago is smooth," I said. "Aged is crumbly. You sprinkle it on salads and soups and pasta."

When I opened my eyes again, Jim was smiling. But he wasn't done with me yet. "Neufchâtel," he said.

I concentrated. Food was something I liked, even if I wasn't very good at preparing it. If I thought of Neufchâtel simply as something to eat, rather than as an ingredient . . .

"Soft and slightly crumbly," I said, and when Jim's eyes lit, I was inordinately proud of myself. "I know the rind is edible, and that some people say the cheese tastes like mushrooms. Sometimes it's called farmers' cheese."

"One more." He narrowed his eyes, and I knew he was going to try to stump me. "Mizithra."

That nearly did me in. But hey, I might not be much of a cook, but that doesn't mean I give up easily. For some reason, his mention of the Greek cheese made me think of the mountain of invoices currently on the desk in my office. A lightbulb went off and I beamed at Jim. "You just ordered some," I said. "A lot, in fact. Mizithra is made from sheep or goat milk. You can serve it as an appetizer with olives or tomatoes, or as a dessert with honey. Or you can serve it with pasta. With the amount you ordered, I'm thinking that you're adding it to the menu."

"In pasta and as a dessert." He made me a showy bow. "You know far more about food than you give yourself credit for. And as a reward for answering all my questions right, I'll prepare some of each cheese for you to take to the wine tasting with you." He moved toward the big industrial refrigerator that took up most of one wall of the kitchen. "A nice platter of Asiago and Neufchâtel with fresh fruit and some crusty bread. How does that sound? And I've been looking for an excuse to make some mizithropita. Mizithra with butter and honey, baked in phyllo. Sound good?"

He knew anything made with honey and phyllo was

right up my alley. I knew that we were done talking about food when Jim's expression grew serious.

"I've talked to Alex's attorney," he said. "A trial date's been set."

Talk of a trial made what Alex was going through all too real. I felt guilty for worrying about my cooking skills (or lack of them) when we had something so much more serious to think about. I wrapped my arms around myself. "And bail?"

Jim's mouth pulled into a frown. "No luck. But the attorney—Melanie—she says she's going to keep trying. If Alex surrenders his passport and I vouch for him, she says there's a chance he'll be able to make the wedding."

"But that's not good enough, is it?" There was a high stool nearby and, suddenly feeling drained, I leaned back against it. "I want to have Alex here for the wedding, of course, but—"

"Did somebody say the magic word?" I swear, Eve has radar when it comes to talking about weddings. She burst into the kitchen looking like a ray of sunshine in a lemon yellow taffeta dress with a swingy skirt and spaghetti straps. It wasn't what she'd been wearing last time I saw her out in the restaurant, and I realized that sometime after we'd locked the front door, she must have ducked into my office to change her clothes. That could only mean one thing—Eve had a date.

"Perfect timing!" she crooned. "The wedding is exactly what I wanted to talk to you both about."

"Er . . ." I looked to Jim for guidance, but since he knew better than to try and put the brakes on Eve—or to get between two best friends—he grabbed a nearby towel and pretended to be busy wiping off the stove even though Marc had already cleaned it and it was spotless. I knew I was on my own. "We weren't talking about the wedding," I told Eve. "Not exactly, anyway. We were talking about Alex."

"Oh, pshaw!" Eve can get away with saying things like that. She's a former beauty queen with a honey-thick Southern accent. When she tossed her head, her blonde hair gleamed in the overhead lights. "I'm not the least little bit worried about Alex. You're going to take care of that, Annie. By the time the wedding rolls around, we'll all be laughing about this crazy mix-up. You're going to prove who really killed that poor woman and Alex won't ever have to think about this whole mess ever again."

"I'm glad you have that much faith in me. I'm just not sure—"

"Of course you are." Eve waved away my protests with one perfectly manicured hand. "You always work things out. You're not going to let Alex down. I know that, Annie. So does Jim and everyone else. That's why we can worry about other things. Like . . ." She took a deep breath and looked from one of us to the other. Why did I have a feeling I wasn't going to like whatever it was Eve said? "Wedding favors!"

"We've talked about that. Jim and I thought—"

"Oh, I know what you thought. You thought you'd give something small and tasteful to every guest. A candle shaped like a wedding cake maybe. Or an African violet plant. That's all well and good. For an ordinary wedding. But then I got to thinking, and what I was thinking was, who's going to remember a wedding where what they get is a small and tasteful favor?"

"So we're talking big and not in good taste?"

Eve was on a roll so she ignored Jim's comment. She

reached into the Kate Spade bag she had on one shoulder and pulled out what looked like a spiral-bound—

"Calendar?" Call me slow, but I couldn't put the concept of calendar and wedding favor together. I stared at her in wonder.

"Not just any calendar. I had a special sample made." Smiling with every ounce of beauty-queen charm she had, Eve flipped open the calendar. Open, it was bigger than a regular piece of copy paper, maybe twenty inches tall by eleven or so inches wide. She happened to open it to the page that showed July. On one page, the dates were marked with boxes. The other page was a picture of Eve's pup Doc in a swimsuit and little terry-cloth beach cover-up. Eve was so excited, she could barely keep still. "Every month features a picture of Doc. Isn't it adorable?"

"It is. He is." A smile pasted to my face, I reached for the calendar and paged through it. In August, Doc was dressed in back-to-school duds. He even had a backpack. September showed him in an apple orchard. He was wearing overalls and a straw hat. Predictably, in October, he was dressed in a Halloween costume, a little red devil, complete with horns. "This is—"

"I know. Brilliant!" Eve sparkled as only Eve can. "Everyone's going to love it, because everyone loves Doc. And look . . ." She plucked the calendar out of my hands and flipped through the pages. "Here in April, the date of your wedding is marked so that everyone remembers your anniversary. And Doc . . ." She made a little *ta-da* gesture to show off the picture of Doc in a tux. Where she'd found another Japanese terrier owner to go along with the plan, I don't know, but there was another dog in the picture. She was dressed like a bride.

"Annie . . ." From behind me, Jim's voice simmered somewhere between *heaven help me* and *you tell her or I will*.

I got the message. "It's so sweet," I said, and really, it was. "But Jim and I, we want to keep things low-key, and you know, giving a favor that cute, it's going to upstage the rest of the wedding."

Eve hadn't thought of this. Her enthusiasm melted in front of my eyes. "You mean—"

"I mean, Doc is so adorable. And all the pictures of him are adorable. But—and don't take this the wrong way—but I—"

"You want to be the center of attention that day! Of course." Eve couldn't believe she hadn't thought of this sooner. "And Doc is so cute—"

"He'd take all the attention away from me. Away from us." I wasn't going to let Jim off the hook. I grabbed his hand and dragged him over to stand beside me. "You understand, don't you?"

"Of course I do, honey." After another quick flip through the pages of the calendar, Eve tucked it back in her purse. "It was silly of me not to think of it in the first place. You're the bride. Everyone should be watching you. Once Doc walks in with the ring on a little satin pillow—"

"No." I couldn't be clearer. I'd already tried beating around the bush, and Eve wasn't listening. "No Doc. No pillow."

"But, Annie—" Luckily, we heard a pounding on the front door, and Eve went to answer. When she swooshed back into the kitchen, she had Tyler with her.

We exchanged hellos and Jim got back to work. There's a lot of cleanup and organization that goes on in a restaurant when the doors close for the night.

Left to my own devices, I closed in on Tyler. There were some things I'd been meaning to ask him, and yeah, I realized the chances of him giving me a straight answer were slim to none. But like I said, I don't give up easily.

"I hear there was an anonymous tip and that's how you found Vickie Monroe's body in that alley."

He wasn't surprised I'd ambushed him with the comment. Tyler rolled back on his heels. "You did your homework."

"But I don't have the answers to all my questions. Like who made the call." Pleading, I looked at him. "If we knew that—"

"If we knew that, we'd know a whole lot more about what happened in that alley."

Encouraged, I jumped on his comment. "Which means you don't think we do know what happened in that alley. Not all of it, anyway. You think we're right, don't you, Tyler? You don't believe Alex killed that woman any more than we do."

One hand out flat and at the level of my nose, he distanced himself from the thought. "I never said that. I just said I'd like more answers."

"And you're not getting them."

"It's not my case."

It wasn't what he said, it was the way he said it. I looked at Tyler hard. "You don't think the detective who's handling the case is doing a good job."

"Derek Harold never does a good job." It was more open than Tyler usually was with me. That told me how frustrated he was by the situation. So did the way he twitched his shoulders, like just thinking about Derek Harold made him want to hop right out of his skin. "Harold takes everything at face value. The man has no imagination. He can't see past what's right in front of his nose."

"Like Alex being in that alley with the victim."

"Well, it is a little hard to ignore that fact." Tyler scraped a hand through his short-cropped, sandy hair. "And yes, the whole thing is driving me crazy. That's why I made some inquiries. I heard talk around the office about the tip, see, and it got me to wondering. Seems the call was made from a public phone a couple blocks away, over at the corner of North Glebe and Seventh Street North."

"Which means some well-meaning passerby may have seen Alex and the victim, panicked, and ran. Then once he—or she—came to his—or her—senses, and he—or . . ." Tyler knew what I meant; I didn't have to elaborate. "Once the person who saw Alex and Vickie in that alley realized what had happened, he called in the tip."

"That's the simplest explanation. And it's probably what happened, but—"

That one little word raised my hopes higher than they had been since Jim got that first call from Alex. I took a few steps closer to Tyler. "But?"

He breathed a sigh of surrender, and I knew why. Tyler doesn't like showing any signs of weakness and, to him, letting me in on what he was thinking was a little too close to actually asking for help. And asking for help . . . well, to Tyler's way of thinking, that definitely was a weakness.

I knew I was right when he latched on to my arm and dragged me over near the back door that led into the alley where Jim parked his motorcycle. Jim was still busy cleaning up and Eve was in the middle of showing the Doc calendar to Marc, but Tyler checked over his shoulder anyway to make sure no one could hear us.

"You've got to help me out here, Annie. Eve is so worried about this whole thing . . ." He checked over his shoulder again and lowered his voice. "She's making me crazy. You know how she can be. She's taken all her worries about Alex and sort of transferred them. You know what I mean? She's obsessed. With your wedding. And if we don't do something fast to calm her down . . ."

I thought of the Doc calendar. I thought about Eve's plans for Fi and Richard's girls, and about the champagne fountain. I knew Tyler was right. Not only did we need to help Alex, but we needed to de-stress Eve. Fast. Before my own wedding was completely out of my control.

And we had a dog as a ring bearer.

Just thinking about it made me woozy, so I concentrated on the case instead. "You think the phone call is suspicious?" I asked Tyler.

"I think . . ." He ordered his thoughts. "If the person who placed that call was nothing but an innocent bystander who just happened on the scene, that person would have stayed around. Or at least shown up at the station later. That's what usually happens. They think about it, they know they have to do the right thing, they come clean and show up and admit they made the call."

"But that's not what happened in this case."

"You got that right," Tyler grumbled. "If Derek Harold wasn't such a bonehead, he'd see what this means."

"And what this means is . . ."

"Well, any idiot can see that," he said, and then when he realized he'd just called me an idiot without actually calling me an idiot, he had the good sense to blush, but, Tyler being Tyler, not the good manners to apologize. "It means the person who placed the call is probably the person who killed Vickie Monroe. The killer wanted us to find Alex with the body."

Hope sprang in my heart. Tyler and I were on the same page! Before I could let my relief get carried away, I stuck with the facts. "And that person wanted you to find Alex with Vickie so it would look like Alex was the killer." Tyler and I eyed each other for a couple seconds, and I knew he was thinking what I was thinking: It was so unusual for us to agree about a case—any case—that he was wondering where to go from here. So was I, so I went for the obvious. "Is there any way you can take over the case?" I asked.

His cynical laugh was the only answer I needed. "Is there any way," Tyler asked, "that you could talk to the husband? You know, get us some firsthand information so that I don't have to accept what Detective Harold says? I swear, the man wouldn't know his head from a—"

I wasn't as worried about Detective Harold as I was about Edward Monroe. That was why I interrupted. "He's a suspect?" I asked, then clarified. "Edward Monroe? You think he—"

Tyler's mouth thinned. "The husband's always a suspect. And I hear he's got an alibi, but I'm just not buying it. The whole thing's a little too convenient. She was stepping out on him, and she ends up dead. It's every husband's dream come true."

I flinched. "That's a cynical view of marriage."

"It's a fact. Most victims are murdered by people they know, and if they're married . . ."

"Then it's usually the spouse who did it." I might not like what Tyler was saying, but I nodded my understanding. "Edward has an alibi?"

"Says he was at a soccer league meeting."

"Then the people he was there with must have con-firmed that." Tyler didn't say a thing. He didn't have to. The police weren't about to accept an alibi without checking it every which way and backward. I came at the problem from another angle. "And you think Edward has a motive because he knew about Vickie and Alex."

"He thought she was going to a cooking class every Tuesday night."

"With her friends." This tallied. Sort of. "But if her friends were at the cooking class and Vickie wasn't there with them . . ." I made a mental note to myself.

"Her friends say that lately, she had excuses for not going to class every Tuesday," Tyler told me. "She wasn't feeling well. One of the kids was sick. She was too busy, too tired."

"But you're not buying it."

Without making it look like he was surrendering to confusion, Tyler shrugged. "I'm not sure it adds up. If you could talk to Vickie Monroe's friends, if you could chat up her husband . . . well, maybe they wouldn't give you the pat answers they're giving us. If Edward Monroe found out Vickie wasn't where she was supposed to be . . . if he found out she was really over at Swallows with Alex . . ."

Again, I nodded. "I wonder why her friends never bothered to mention it to me," I said, talking more to myself than to Tyler. I knew he wasn't following so I filled him in. "They told me that Vickie never would have snuck around behind Edward's back. But they never mentioned that she'd missed cooking classes. They knew she wasn't with them when they went to Sonny's on Tuesday nights and she must have missed plenty of classes. She went to Swallows more than once. So what did her friends think she was up to?"

It was a very good question, and I intended to find the answer.

Before I left Bellywasher's, I let Jim know I would gladly take him up on the offer of the cheese platter and the Greek dessert.

After all, designated cooking expert or not, I was going to a wine tasting, and I couldn't go empty-handed.

Seven

✖

BETH AND MICHAEL'S HOUSE WAS EVEN MORE elegant than the brick Colonial I imagined for myself. It was sprawling and modern, with lots of windows, clean lines, and a roof sloped at impossible angles. The yard was a match for the house, neat without being severe, landscaped with just the right amount of shrubs to be interesting without being overdone or overwhelming. In fact, the one and only concession to hominess was a too cute *Welcome Friends* sign on a post stuck into the flower bed near the front door. The sign was shaped like a giant egg and made out of weatherproof resin. The smiling, waving bear and moose on the sign looked as out of place in the gee-whiz neighborhood as I felt.

Beth welcomed me inside, and I saw that the house had an open, airy foyer with a ceramic tile floor in a shade of ecru that appealed to my love of all colors neutral and my sense of decorating restraint. Just inside the front door and at the bottom of a winding staircase, the wall to my left was made from glass block and lit from bchind. Set in front of it on see-through shelves was a collection of art glass that took my breath away.

At the risk of being rude, I couldn't take my eyes off the vases and plates in various shapes and sizes and in a riot of blue, red, green, purple, and orange. Yeah, my mouth was hanging open, but I managed to gasp, "I'm not a fan of lots of color, but that's just spectacular."

Perfect hostess that she was, she smiled and thanked me. "The glass is Michael's baby," she said. "He's the collector. I just go along with whatever he wants. That, and take out the feather duster when it all needs cleaning!"

I was so fascinated, I was being rude. I shook myself back to the present, remembered the bottle of wine I'd picked up at Très Bonne Cuisine and the darling gift bag Norman had chosen for it, one with the Eiffel Tower on it. "For you," I said, handing the bag to Beth. It was the first I registered that she was a riot of color that Friday evening, too, in a floral print sundress as cheery as the daffodils that grew around the front door. "The wine is a zinfandel, just like you asked for. And here . . ." I'd brought the cheese plate and the mizithra, honey, and phyllo dessert in a carry bag and I gave that to her, too. "My contribution to the nibblers."

"But no husband? We were looking forward to meeting him." Wineglass in hand, Celia appeared from around the corner and looked over the scene. She was wearing silky black pants and a flowing black top that made my khakis and powder blue sweater look positively passé. "No problem if he can't come until later. Our guys aren't here yet, either, but they'll be along eventually. You know how traffic is this time of the day."

"Jim's out of town on business!" I'd practiced the phrase in the car (and not incidentally, I'd borrowed Norman's silver Jag for the occasion), and delivered it in a way that made it sound like *again!* even though I didn't say it. "He sends his best and says he hopes to meet everyone next time. Oh!" I didn't have to pretend to be embarrassed. If I wasn't on a case and hadn't come there specifically to try to get people to talk, I'd never dream of being that rude. "I mean, if we're invited next time."

"Of course you're invited. We're neighbors!" Glynis came from the back of the house. She was wearing a linen apron embroidered with spring violets over a pantsuit in an ashen color that matched her hair. She wound an arm through mine and gave it a squeeze. "And next time, you can bring those adorable girls of yours, too. The kids are playing upstairs." Just as she said this, we heard a sound like thunder from upstairs. One of the doors along the hallway at the top of the steps flew open and a troop of children raced from one room to another. I recognized Beth's Jeremy, Glynis's Eli, and Carter, the soccer star. There were a couple older girls with them as well as three older boys I didn't know and Vickie Monroe's Henry and Antonia.

"Oh, Edward's going to be here?" It was, of course, exactly what I was hoping for, so I tried not to look too pleased with myself. "I thought—"

"He'll be along after work," Beth said. "His kids came home from school with mine."

"He needs to relax," Glynis said.

"He needs to be with friends," Celia added.

"And Edward has to be here. He's got an announcement to make, and we've all got something to celebrate," Beth said rather cryptically, and when her friends questioned her, she put a finger to her lips. "You'll all find out soon enough," she said in that singsong sort of way people do when they can't wait to spill a secret.

Before any of us had a chance to say another word, the kids raced across the second-floor landing again.

"If you all settle down, you can go down to the media room and watch your movie," Beth called up to them. "If not . . ."

The unspoken threat was enough to bring them in line instantly. They streamed down the steps, and Glynis told them to stop in the kitchen on their way to the media room. She had popcorn, sodas, and cookies all ready for them.

"Mine, mine, mine," Beth said, patting the heads of Jeremy as well as two girls who looked to be twins. "You know Eli," she said, pointing out Glynis's son, "and these are her Isabelle and Connor." The little girl ignored me; the boy smiled and turned pink.

"And these are my Jackson and Mitchell," Celia added. They were clearly the oldest kids there and even though I wasn't a mother, I knew exactly what Celia was going to say next. "Keep an eye on the little ones," she told her sons. "No roughhousing! And if anyone spills anything—"

"We know," the oldest boy rolled his eyes in a way that said he wasn't being disrespectful so much as he was just teasing. He'd heard it all before. "Wipe it up and let you know if there's a stain."

"Beautiful kids," I said, because it was true and because I know that's what mothers are supposed to say to each other.

Glynis still had a hold of my arm. She tugged me toward the kitchen and I just naturally went along. "I suppose you're wondering why we asked you to come so early," she said.

"Sonny made flan in cooking class this week," Celia added, though what this had to do with me arriving early

MURDER HAS A SWEET TOOTH

for the wine tasting, I don't know. "Flan Caraqueño. It's a recipe from Venezuela."

"And Celia . . ." Beth slid her friend a look. "Celia mentioned it to Michael. Michael loves flan. And since the celebration has something to do with Michael . . ."

Again her friends questioned her, but again, Beth clammed up like a . . . well, like a clam. We trooped into the kitchen (where I didn't see a trace of flan) and Beth bustled to the refrigerator and took out eggs, butter, and milk. She set it on the quartz countertop while Celia brought over almonds and crackers, and Glynis went into a walk-in pantry as big as the kitchen in my apartment to get a bottle of vanilla extract.

"Thing is," Beth said, "Michael doesn't like flan when it's really cold. You know, the way you usually get it when you order it in a restaurant. Go figure. He's got this weird thing about flan. He likes it when it's had just enough time to chill to set up."

"That's . . . nice." I didn't know what else to say.

"We'll serve it after the appetizers and the wine," Celia informed me. At the same time she grabbed a green linen apron embroidered with bunnies and looped it over my head. "You know, when we bring out the coffee."

"What a surprise!" Beth clapped her hands together in excitement. "Fresh flan, and not too cold. Just the way Michael likes it!" Beth was smiling when she ducked around behind me to tie the apron strings behind my back.

And me? I was standing in the middle of the kitchen, feeling a little like Cinderella in that cartoon scene where the mice get her dressed for the ball. Like those mice, Celia, Glynis, and Beth stepped back and gave me their nodding approval.

I plucked at the apron. "I would have brought my own, but—"

"No need!" Beth's smile was a mile wide. "No problem at all with you using one of mine. I mean, it's the least we can do for you."

I looked from one woman to the other. I might have been more encouraged if they weren't all smiling. "It's the least you can do for me because I'm going to . . ."

Celia laughed. "You're going to make the flan, of course."

My heart thudded to my toes, then bounced up again. It wedged in my throat. At the same time I scrambled for something to say that might save me from the fate worse than death, I told myself I'd never believe Jim MacDonald again. Not ever again. He was the one who assured me there would be no cooking involved in tonight's festivities. And now that I thought about it, he was the one who'd been too busy at Bellywasher's to come along. If he had taken a couple hours off and joined me in McLean, I would have gladly given over the apron to him and he would have just as gladly produced a flan to be proud of. Me?

I didn't have the strength to even think about it.

Automatically, I reached around my back to untie the apron. "I really don't think this is a good idea. I mean—"

"But you said you took classes at Très Bonne Cuisine," Glynis protested.

Beth pouted. "And flan *is* Michael's favorite."

I forced myself to smile while I tried to think of a way out, and while I was still smiling, a sneaky suspicion formed in my mind: Celia, Glynis, and Beth all loved to cook. I knew this because they all took classes at Sonny's. If I was going to be one of the crowd, I had to prove

I loved to cook, too. And if I was going to find out anything about Vickie Monroe's life—and more importantly, her death—I had to be one of the crowd.

Since my hands were still behind my back, it was no effort at all to cross my fingers when I announced, "Flan just happens to be one of my specialties."

HERE'S THE THING ABOUT FLAN: IT DOESN'T HAVE very many ingredients. That meant when I looked over the recipe Beth handed me, it all seemed pretty straightforward. A second look, though, and the all-too-familiar rat-a-tat of culinary doubt started up inside my brain. There's this whole process of caramelizing sugar in a pan, see, and then coating the pan with the caramelized sugar, and then baking the custardy flan in the caramelized pan while the flan in the caramelized pan is set in another pan of hot water.

Just thinking about it leaves me light-headed and out of breath.

Sure, Jim could have done it with his eyes closed. Norman could have produced a magnificent flan with his hands tied behind his back. Even Eve, who had proved herself a better cook than either of us would have imagined before that fateful class as Très Bonne Cuisine, probably could have made something if not incredible, then at least edible.

Annie Capshaw? Not so much.

After three tries (and a whole lot of wasted sugar), I finally got the pan caramelized. Only I don't think caramelized sugar is supposed to be the color of a used tire.

I got the almonds and the cracker crumbs and the eggs and everything else mixed together, too. And if the dropped egg, the spilled milk, and the bottle of vanilla extract I knocked over doesn't count, it all went without a hitch.

Finally, with the flan in the oven, Celia, Glynis, Beth, and I sipped wine and sampled the appetizers they were setting out on fancy plates so they'd be ready to serve when the husbands arrived. And when my flan came out of the oven, lopsided and smelling scorched, here's the really amazing thing . . .

Nobody cared!

Celia, Glynis, and Beth really were as gracious as could be! They didn't criticize, they didn't complain. They didn't critique my cooking technique (or lack of it). They simply complimented me, assured me that the guys (Michael especially) would be over the moon at such a wonderful dessert, and cooed and clucked over the flan as if they'd been the proud layers of the eggs that went into it.

The men arrived from their high-powered jobs and I was introduced all around. Beth's husband, Michael, sprinted upstairs the moment he was through the front door, and when he reappeared, he was wearing a cotton sweater that perfectly matched the yellow in her sundress. Celia's Scott was as quiet as he was tall and thin. Glynis and Howard (who everyone called Chip) barely kissed each other hello before Chip dived into two big glasses of wine in very short order. With barely more than a nod of his head, Edward Monroe acknowledged me, then disappeared into the great room with the rest of the guys.

"I'll bet they're already starting in on the hokey-pokeys. That's what Sonny made in cooking class last week," Beth confided with a wink at her friends. "The guys love them."

Apparently, they did. By the time we walked into the spacious great room with its leather furniture and floor-to-ceiling windows, the women's husbands were gathered around a table, chowing down from a plate of appetizers that included slices of little party bread loaded with what looked like sausage and melted cheese. Beth set down the fruit and cheese platter I'd brought and they dug into that, too. Edward Monroe, I noticed, was on the other side of the room, sipping a glass of bloodred wine and staring out the window.

When she was done making sure everything was perfect (need I mention that it was?), Beth turned to Edward. "Now that everything is ready, we can have our toast," she said, and when he didn't respond right away, she added, "Edward, you did want to offer a toast, didn't you?"

Without a word, he came over to where we were gathered and I had a chance to look him over. That Friday night, Edward didn't look a thing like the go-get-'em coach I'd seen at the soccer game. Unlike Scott and Chip, who'd discarded their expensive suit coats and loosened their Italian silk ties, Edward was buttoned up and buttoned down. All business, no casual. He was a good-looking guy, a little older than me, with dark hair shot with gray. His face was drawn and lined; his eyes were unfocused. He looked exactly like what he was, a man whose wife had been horribly taken from him, and before I could go and get all mushy about it, I reminded myself of my conversation with Tyler just the night before.

It's always the husband.

Those might not have been Tyler's exact words, but they were close enough. And chilling, too. Was Edward Monroe heartless enough to murder his wife and pin it on a stranger? I didn't know, but I needed to find out.

I reminded myself to stay objective and watched while Edward set down his glass of wine and reached for a bottle of champagne that had been tucked into an ice bucket out of sight of the wine tasters. He showed the label to Beth, who nodded her approval, and then he popped the cork. Beth had crystal champagne flutes ready, and as Edward filled the glasses, she passed them around. When she got to Michael, she whispered something in his ear. His cheeks got dusky.

Beth held her glass in front of her with both hands. "I'm going to let Edward do the honors," she said.

Call it my imagination running away with me, but I had the distinct feeling that Edward would have rather done just about anything but. He swallowed hard and cleared his throat. "I suppose you're all wondering why I've called you here today," he said, and we all laughed on cue. He didn't smile when we all did, so his expression didn't exactly *get* serious. It got *more* serious. Determined. I had a feeling that if I was standing next to him, I would have heard the bones in his jaw grind together. When he finally forced a smile, the corners of his mouth were as stiff as my meringue never was. "Since this is a surprise to most of you, I'll explain that I called Michael into my office this afternoon." With his champagne flute, he gestured toward Beth's husband. "Michael's been . . . well, he's been a real asset to the company. I've known him since I purchased Macro-Tech seven years ago, and I can say with some authority that we wouldn't be where we are today without him leading the charge down in the accounting department. You know I'm much too obsessive to ever loosen my hold on the reins of the company completely, but since everything that happened to Vickie . . . well, I'd like to back off a bit, to free up some time for the kids. I'm happy to tell all of you that as of this afternoon, Macro-Tech has a new chief financial officer." Edward raised his glass. "To Michael!"

At the announcement, the women squealed their delight and hugged Beth. After they drank down their champagne, the men offered Michael their congratulations and handshakes.

"That's great news," I said to Beth, and honestly, I don't know if she heard me since she was so busy beaming a mile-wide smile at her husband. Michael, too, was looking pretty starry-eyed. Who could blame him? I might not be a mover or shaker when it comes to big business, but I'd done my homework. Macro-Tech was Edward Monroe's software firm, and it was a mighty successful one at that. The company handled any number of huge government contracts, and unlike a lot of businesses these days, his always turned a profit. Macro-Tech had made Edward millions. It was nice to see he was sharing the wealth, and even nicer to know that Beth had a husband who was well-thought-of enough to be handed the new responsibility. I couldn't help but be as pleased as everyone else. I sipped my champagne, enjoying the moment.

At least until I realized that in spite of the fact that Edward's toast had been gracious, his expression never changed. For a man who was loosening his hold—just a bit—on his company, to spend more time with his motherless children, he didn't look relieved, happy, or even content.

I was curious. And like it or not, thanks to everything I'd been through since that first, fateful cooking class I took and that first murder I'd solved, I was suspicious, too. First Jeremy, the kid who gave nonathletic a whole new meaning, was playing soccer. Then Michael gets a promotion? Sure, I knew good things happened to nice people, and from what I'd seen, Beth and Michael and the rest of them were really nice people. Still, it all seemed a little too fishy.

Eager to find out if my detective instincts were right on, or if I was just letting my imagination run wild, I leaned toward Beth so I could whisper, "It's such good news and it makes so much sense for Edward to take some time to recuperate from everything that's happened. I wonder why he doesn't look happier about it."

I hoped for a reaction. But not one that involved the need for a cleanup crew.

No such luck. Beth winced as if she'd been slapped, the blood drained from her face, and, as if in slow motion, her champagne glass slipped out of her hands.

Eight

✴

BETH'S CRYSTAL CHAMPAGNE FLUTE HIT THE COR-
ner of the table and from there, the hardwood
floor. Champagne rained down on everything, and the
glass shattered into a million pieces.

"I'm so sorry." No, it wasn't exactly my fault. Or
maybe it was since I'd apparently startled Beth with my
comment. Whatever the case, to prove how awful I felt,
I set down my own glass and went into the kitchen. There
were bound to be paper towels in there, and a broom and
a dustpan, too.

Of course, finding everything in a kitchen the size
of my apartment was no easy thing. I finally took a chance
on the walk-in pantry where, earlier, Glynis had gotten the
vanilla extract. Success! I found a roll of paper towels.

I was just about to head back into the great room,
when a stack of magazines on the kitchen desk caught
my eye. They were cooking magazines and—do I need
to say it?—cooking magazines usually send chills up my
spine. Except the magazine on top had a headline across

the front of it that said, "Foods of Scotland." Honestly, all I meant to do was take a peek and get some kind of idea for a wedding dinner surprise that didn't involve skinning fish or cooking their heads in seawater.

But when I heard someone coming, I suddenly felt guilty for paging through Beth's magazine. Maybe because I felt guilty about being in her home under false pretenses? Psychology aside, I caught sight of the carry bag I'd brought along with me, and automatically tucked the magazine inside it. By the time Celia walked into the kitchen, I was standing there holding the paper towels and trying not to look like the thief I felt I was.

"Paper towels." As if she couldn't see them, I held them up. "I can't believe what a mess I made in there."

"You didn't do a thing. Don't worry about it. Drinks spill. Glasses break. Besides, Beth's walking on a cloud. She couldn't care less about any of it."

Just as I'm sure Celia intended, this made me feel better. While she gathered up a broom and a dustpan from just inside the laundry room, I took the chance of sticking my nose just a little further into these people's lives. "Beth's very proud of Michael, isn't she?" I asked, as innocent as can be. "And Michael must be thrilled to take on such a prominent position. I wonder why Edward doesn't look the least bit happy about any of it."

Celia shook her head and clicked her tongue. "I swear, the man has lost his mind. I guess it's only natural. I mean, considering what happened to Vickie and all. I just don't understand—"

"What?"

Her gaze darted to the doorway, and seeing that no one was around, she stepped closer and lowered her voice. "First he lets Jeremy play in the soccer game. Now it's Michael's promotion. It doesn't make sense."

"Because Jeremy's a lousy soccer player, and Michael . . . ?" I held my breath and waited for her to say more.

She did. But not until after she'd looked at the doorway again. "A couple weeks ago, Beth called me in tears. There was a rumor going around Macro-Tech and she caught wind of it from Michael's administrative assistant. Something about Michael screwing up a really big account. Beth was worried sick because there was talk of Michael being let go."

"And today, he was named CFO." This was curious, and I chewed over the thought for a moment while I drummed my fingers against my chin. "Maybe," I suggested, "Edward found out it was all a big mistake. You know, about Michael messing up that account. Maybe he's trying to make it up to Michael."

Celia shook her head. "Edward isn't the type to kiss and make up. Not with anybody. You don't get that powerful by being a marshmallow."

"Then maybe he's just feeling warm and fuzzy. You know, because of Vickie."

"That's it. That's got to be it." Celia was relieved. She backed off. "I'd better take care of that glass in there before Beth feels she has to. I don't want to spoil her celebration."

"I don't, either." I clasped the roll of paper towels to my chest. "But there's one other thing . . ."

If Celia was less polite, she would have ignored me. The way it was, she stopped in midstride, broom in one hand, dustpan in the other, and looked at me over her shoulder.

As casually as I could, I said, "Edward thought Vickie was going to cooking class on Tuesday nights."

Big points for Celia, her expression never changed.

But I couldn't help but notice that her slender shoulders went rigid.

When she didn't say a word, I knew I had to. "Vickie's been hanging around at Swallows on Tuesday nights for a few weeks now. You all go to cooking class on Tuesday nights and Vickie was supposed to be with you. But I bet she had excuses, right? She didn't feel well. She was busy. Once, I can see, and you'd never question it. Twice, it happens, and you offer to help out if she's so overwhelmed she can't take care of things by herself. But I think after three times, her friends would start asking questions."

"Hurry up with that broom, Celia!" Glynis called from the great room. It was a perfect excuse for Celia to cut and run, and cut and run she did. I was left with unanswered questions.

Of course, I had every intention of finding out more before I left there that night.

With that in mind, I had just stepped out of the kitchen door when I ran smack into Edward Monroe. Good thing I had that roll of paper towels clutched to my chest. It cushioned the blow.

"I'm so sorry." At the same time that I automatically smoothed the wrinkle the paper towel roll put in his tie, I stepped back into the kitchen. "I didn't see you come around the corner."

"No problem." Edward didn't say this in a tone of voice any different from the one he'd used when he was praising Michael to the high heavens. "Didn't want to leave a mess for Beth and Michael." He held up his glass for me to see. It was empty. "I need to head out."

"But the kids aren't done with their movie." I didn't need to be a mother to know this would be a major bone of contention.

"They're staying here tonight but I've got to run." Edward crossed the room and put his glass in the sink. "Beth invited them, and I think it will be good for them to be with their friends for the evening." He took a step toward the doorway and I had not one doubt that he was going to say his good-byes and leave for home.

I sidestepped my way in front of him. "That's really nice. Beth and Celia and Glynis, they were good friends to Vickie."

"Yes, they were." For the first time, Edward actually took the time to look me over. Apparently, I wasn't all that interesting, because it didn't take all that long. "It was nice meeting you, Annie," he said in the perfunctory way people do when they just want to get something over with. "Maybe I'll see you again sometime."

My smile was as brief as my pretending to go along with the pretended niceness. "Before you leave . . ." I wormed my way directly into Edward's path again. "There's just something I wanted to ask you about. Just something I was wondering."

I can't say he was thrilled about being cornered. But he was nothing if not polite. Edward waited semipatiently.

And I wondered how I could ease my way into asking what I needed to ask, and then realized there was no way, and I might as well just get it over with. "I was just wondering . . ." I smiled. Decided I was being too sociable. Wiped my expression clean. "Celia, Glynis, and Beth go to cooking classes every Tuesday evening," I said.

Edward didn't so much shrug as twitch his shoulders, as if he could barely be bothered with what was bothering me. "I'm sure they'd let you tag along." He moved to his left.

I angled myself to my right. "I'm sure they would.

Only I don't want to. And apparently, Vickie didn't want to, either."

He went as still as a statue.

I held my breath.

This time when Edward looked me over, he took his time. Maybe he'd decided I wasn't so easy to dismiss after all. But before I could figure out if this was a good thing or a bad thing, he backed up a step, cocked his head, and said, "You didn't even know Vickie. Why do you care?"

I knew it would come to this. How could it not?

Have I mentioned that in real life I'm a completely honest person, but that when it comes to an investigation, I sometimes have to compromise my honesty and I do it without even a hint of guilt?

I did it right then and there. "It's so glaring," I said. "I mean, I can't believe the cops haven't asked you. Well, I bet they have!" I laughed because right about then, Edward looked like a volcano that was about to blow, and I knew I needed to defuse the situation—and fast. I morphed from superserious to embarrassed in no time flat.

"It's none of my business. Of course it's none of my business," I stammered. "It's just that no one's said a word about it, and I was wondering, that's all. If Celia, Glynis, and Beth were at cooking class, they obviously would have noticed that Vickie wasn't at cooking class. I mean, they must have, right? And we know Vickie wasn't at cooking class because she was over at that restaurant in Arlington with that guy. And the night she was—" I couldn't take the chance of alienating Edward completely. I carefully avoided the *m* word. Talk of murder tends to make people queasy. Especially when they're spouses.

Or suspects.

"The night that everything happened, that wasn't the first night Vickie was in Arlington with that man. At least that's what I read in the papers. And that means she'd missed more than just a couple cooking classes, and if she missed a couple cooking classes, of course, her friends would have noticed. And they would have asked her about it, of course. I mean, I certainly would ask a friend where she'd been if I thought she was going to be one place and she didn't show up. And they did, and Vickie always had an excuse. So I was just wondering if any of them mentioned it to you. You know, if they asked you if Vickie was feeling better, or if they mentioned how much they missed having her in class with them on Tuesday nights. I just wondered, that's all. I can't help it." I added this final bit because a streak of red had streamed up Edward's neck and stained his cheeks and I was afraid he was going to burst a blood vessel. "I guess I'm just too curious for my own good."

My phony lack of confidence worked! It put Edward at ease. He smiled. In fact, he laughed. He even patted me on the shoulder.

"You're right," he said. "You are too curious for your own good."

And with that, Edward Monroe walked out of the kitchen.

And me?

I stood there clutching that roll of paper towels (they were an expensive brand and plushier than the ones I usually bought, so it was as soothing as hugging a teddy bear) and thinking. And what I thought was pretty jumbled, but what it amounted to was this:

If Edward Monroe was guilty (and Tyler's professional opinion and my gut reaction said he certainly could be), then he'd possibly just threatened me and I probably should be worried.

I would be, too, as soon as I had time.

Right then and there, though, I had bigger things to think about. Like Jeremy playing soccer and Michael, the man who had nearly been sacked just a couple weeks before, being named to a prestigious position in a successful software firm.

See what I'm getting at here?

Even as I walked back into the great room and started sopping up champagne from the tabletop and the floor, I couldn't help but think that Edward Monroe was guilty.

And that Beth knew it.

As far as I could see, that was the only thing that could explain how she was blackmailing him.

I DIDN'T WANT TO SUSPECT EDWARD MONROE. Really. So he wasn't the friendliest guy in the world. So he wasn't Mr. Charm. So statistics say that most murder victims are killed by someone they know and that often, that someone is their spouse. That didn't automatically mean Edward killed Vickie. Did it?

Just thinking about it made me queasy, and I wasn't kidding myself. I knew exactly why. After all, I was getting married in just two short (and getting shorter all the time) weeks, and the life I was planning with Jim was as perfect as my daydreams could make it. Wondering if Vickie and Edward Monroe had once had those kinds of hopes for their marriage and if their love had deteriorated so much that it had exploded into a murderous attack in an alley outside a bar . . .

Well, thinking about it was enough to make this soon-to-be bride wish she wasn't also a private detective.

But I was. A private detective, that is. And I had promised Jim I would clear Alex's name.

With that in mind, I knew what I had to do. I had to search for the truth, and follow the clues—and my instincts—wherever they led. If they brought me to the conclusion that some marriages don't end in happily-ever-after . . . well, I already knew that. After all, I'd once been married to Peter.

But what if my investigation brought me face-to-face with the fact that some not-so-happily-ever-afters also include murder?

Even though I was standing in a pool of sunlight outside the Spring Hill Recreation Center, I shivered. It was the next day, Saturday afternoon, and before I could let my imagination run wild and carry my worries and my common sense away with it, I reminded myself I was there on business. The recreation center was where Edward had his soccer coaches' meeting the night Vickie was murdered, and that meant it was the place I might start to get to the bottom of what happened outside Swallows. I had to stay objective. I owed it to Jim. I owed it to Alex, because if Tyler suspected I was biased in any way, shape, or form, he wouldn't believe a thing I said when it came to proving Alex's innocence. I owed it to Vickie Monroe. Especially to Vickie Monroe, and to her two adorable children, Henry and Antonia, who would grow up without a mother.

Keeping the image of Henry and Antonia firmly in mind, I pulled back my shoulders, marched into the rec center, and offered a broad smile to the middle-aged woman behind the counter. "Annie Capshaw," I said.

"I'm with the McLean Virginia Now! You know, the Web site."

The woman—whose name tag said she was Deb—couldn't have known the site because I made it up. Polite person that she was, she nodded anyway. "How can I help you?" she asked.

I tried my best to look bored. No easy thing when I'm on a case and my brain is buzzing with prospects and possibilities. "My boss is making me do this," I confided, leaning over the desk and lowering my voice. "I mean, who even wants to read an article about a bunch of soccer coaches getting together for a planning meeting? But . . ." My sigh was packed with enough resignation to sound genuine. "If I have to, I have to. I know they met here on . . ." I flipped open the portfolio I was carrying, the better to consult what I hoped looked like reporter-like notes, and gave Deb the date on which Vickie was killed. "I don't need much. You know, just the names of the coaches who were here, which teams they represent, how long the meeting lasted. I guess the idea is that we're supposed to show the community how active the soccer league is. You know, good PR."

Apparently, Deb did know about PR, and since there's nothing top secret about a league meeting for coaches, she wasn't hesitant to share. She did some digging in a file cabinet behind the desk, found what she was looking for, and made a copy for me.

"It's public record," she said, passing the copy of the meeting minutes over the desk to me. "Nothing in there the coaches would object to anyone seeing. Just never had anyone ask before. Didn't think anyone cared."

I assured her McLean Virginia Now! did, and thanked her. As I walked away from the desk and found a seat on a bench near the door, I was already flipping through the minutes. It didn't take long. They spelled out everything I was looking for in a report that was exactly three pages long. Edward Monroe had been at the meeting from the beginning. I knew this, because he offered the first report on the agenda, the one about league finances. He'd been there all the way to the bitter end, too; he seconded the motion to adjourn. According to the times listed in the minutes and to everything Tyler said about how long Vickie had been dead when the police found her body, there was no way Edward could have left the meeting when he did and still driven to Arlington in time to slit his wife's throat.

A wave of relief washed over me, and I can attribute it only to the fact that finding out that Edward could not have been the murderer reaffirmed my faith in marriage. Of course, it did nothing at all for my case.

Thinking it over, I was just about to slip the minutes into my portfolio when I realized someone was standing right in front of the bench where I was seated.

I looked up and found Edward Monroe looking down at me.

"Deb says you're with McLean Virginia Now!"

Deb, much to my dismay, had excellent hearing and a memory for trivial information that was far better than I'd hoped.

I wasn't about to let that stop me. I hopped to my feet and Edward didn't have a lot of choice: It was either step back or invade my personal space. "It's kind of a hobby. You know, just something to pass the time. Jim works so many hours, and he's out of town so often."

"And you're writing an article about the soccer league." He touched a hand to the front of his blue windbreaker with its soccer league emblem above a Tigers patch. "Maybe you'd like to come watch today's game."

Edward looked toward the door and I saw that out on the soccer fields beyond, kids clad in Tigers blue and white were gathering and warming up by kicking soccer balls around. "Reporting on a game, that would add some real color."

My smile was bright as I sidestepped away from Edward. "I wouldn't want to sound biased toward any one team."

"But an article about a coaches' meeting . . ." He countered with a step into my path. "That doesn't sound all that interesting."

"Blame my editor." I hoisted my purse to my shoulder and tucked my portfolio under my arm. "She said she wanted facts and figures."

Edward nodded. He understood. The look he gave me wasn't exactly a smile. "The same facts and figures the police have been asking about."

"Really?" If I'd learned anything from a lifetime of being best friends with Eve, it was how to toss my head in that wow-imagine-that kind of way that always catches guys off guard. Without fail, it works for Eve. For me? Not so much. At least if Edward's stony silence meant anything.

It was one of those awkward moments I'm so not good at. And a chance I might never get again. Determined to get at the truth, I took the proverbial bull by the horns. "I'll bet the police asked something else, too. I bet they asked if you left the meeting for a while. If you were there at the beginning, and there at the end, and if in between—"

"I popped out to murder my wife?" Edward's eyes were blue. The color the Chesapeake Bay turns right before a storm.

I sucked in a breath and held it until my lungs felt as

if they'd burst. That was right about the same time Edward threw back his head and laughed. "You ask a lot of questions, Annie."

"Reporters do that." Ambiguous, but true.

And apparently enough to satisfy Edward. His smile was cordial, but reserved, as if we'd just been introduced at a business meeting. "I can't wait to read your article," he said.

"I'll let you know when it's posted," I promised, and because there wasn't anything else to say and nothing to be gained from a man who was clearly toying with me, I nodded my good-bye and slipped away from him and toward the door.

I didn't breathe a sigh of relief until I was safely outside, and I refused to look back, either, even though I could feel Edward's gaze fastened between my shoulder blades. I marched to my car and unlocked the door. I had already tossed my portfolio inside when a car pulled into the parking place next to time, and Chip, Glynis's husband, got out.

"Hi, Chip." His eyes were unfocused and I could tell he didn't remember me. But then, at Beth's house the night before, it was obvious Chip was more interested in drinking wine than he was in the company of his friends. I'd personally counted seven glasses that he drank, and that was before Beth served my flan with Kahlua and coffee. Just in case he was still a little bleary-eyed (either from the alcohol or from my too-rubbery flan), I rounded his Audi. "I'm Annie. We met last night at Michael and Beth's."

"Of course." His smile came and went quickly. Like Edward, he was wearing a blue Tigers windbreaker and he smoothed one hand over it. "You're new to the neighborhood."

"And I hope I'm fitting in. It's kind of awkward. You know, trying to get to know people. I mean, with all that happened to Vickie . . ." I dragged the thought out, hoping he'd jump right in and fill in some of the gaps. When all he did was shift uncomfortably from foot to foot, I decided on a more direct approach.

"That was great news about Michael. About his promotion. I just saw Edward inside." Almost afraid to look, I turned that way. There was no sign of Edward Monroe, thank goodness. "He's seems really excited about having Michael on board as CFO. He said it's going to take a real load of day-to-day worries off his back."

"He did?" Chip wrinkled his nose and behind his thick glasses, his eyes squinched. "Glynis says—" He caught himself and cleared his throat.

Like all detectives everywhere, I knew exactly what that meant. Chip's common sense had momentarily gotten the best of him. Too bad. Because I would have loved to know what Glynis said about Michael's promotion.

Of course, that didn't mean I couldn't pretend I already did.

"I know. That's what she told me, too." I raised my eyebrows and laughed, sharing the confidence with Chip. "And after all that stuff a couple weeks ago about how Michael almost got fired . . ."

Like I'd done, Chip looked toward the front door of the rec center, and call me too imaginative for my own good, but I swear he was looking for Edward, too, and when he didn't see him, relief swept across his expression. "He never really would have done it," Chip confided. "Edward talks a good game. You know, hard-nosed. But then, he has to, doesn't he? He's running a major corporation and he can't afford any screwups. But when push came to shove, he wouldn't have given Michael his walking papers. Edward's not that kind of guy."

Eager to hear more, I inched forward. "What kind of guy is he?"

"Edward?" Again, Chip glanced over my shoulder toward the rec center. When he looked back at me, I practically heard his smile screech. That's how stiff it was. "Edward's a great guy," he assured me. "He was a loving husband, and he's a good friend. A really good friend. I'd better get to the game," he added, backing away. "The kids are waiting."

It wasn't until he was all the way over at the soccer field that I turned back to my car.

That was when I realized Edward Monroe was standing outside the rec center watching us both.

Nine

BELLYWASHER'S IS CLOSED ON MONDAYS, SO THE next Monday instead of catching up on restaurant paperwork or staying at home to tackle the mountain of laundry waiting for me, I talked Eve into rescheduling her appointment with her aesthetician and I did something I have never done before of my own free will: I went to a cooking store.

And not just any cooking store—Sonny's, in Reston.

We stopped just outside so we could look over the gingham curtains that framed the front window, where stuffed teddy bears dressed as chefs worked at a pint-sized stove, served from teensy silver trays, and sat at a teddy-sized dinner table. "Cute," I decided.

It was. Sonny's shop was not as elegant as Très Bonne Cuisine. It was not as ultramodern or (from what I could see as I stepped inside the front door and took a quick look around) as expensive. What it was, though, was down-home delightful. We stepped inside and into the old-time general-store decor, and saw at once that Sonny's was as country as Très Bonne Cuisine was sophisticated. Jacques . . . er . . . Norman would have hated every inch of it. I, on the other hand, did not feel the least bit intimidated. In fact, I took a deep breath, and was rewarded with the incredible aroma of barbecue. I let that breath out slowly, and I swear I felt the cooking-induced tension that always assails me in such places melt like a pat of butter in a hot pan. "This is the most comfortable and at home I've ever felt in a cooking store," I told Eve. "Even when I did my stint as manager of Très Bonne Cuisine."

Of course, I don't think she heard me. Eve was already checking out a display of party favors, and I had the uneasy feeling we'd be having the wedding souvenir discussion again soon.

No matter. At least not right then. I followed my nose, savoring the scent of barbecue all the while. That shouldn't come as any surprise. I didn't have to be a good cook to have good taste, or to know that good barbecue is right up there on my gotta-have-it list with any form of chocolate, any flavor of cheesecake, and juicy hamburgers—as long as there's a slice of cheddar melted on the top and a side of fries to go with them.

I found myself all the way at the back of the shop and face-to-face with a tall man whose name tag said he was Sonny himself. He was about fifty, broad shouldered, and muscular, with a shock of brown hair, a face that wasn't as handsome as it was agreeable, and eyes as blue as the Virginia sky. There was a slow cooker open on the counter in front of him, and when he leaned over it and breathed in deep, his smile was a mile wide.

"That smells fabulous," I said, and Sonny rewarded me by grabbing a plastic spoon, dipping it into the barbecue sauce that bubbled in the slow cooker, and holding it up to my lips. I tasted and smiled my approval.

"That, darlin', is some of the best barbecue you'll have this side of the Mason-Dixon Line." Sonny's Southern accent was as heavy as his smile was contagious. He grabbed another spoon and took a taste for himself and when he was done, he smacked his lips. "Sonny's Extra-Special Sweet and Tangy Sauce. If I put it on top of my head, my tongue would slap my brains out trying to get at it! We sell it by the pint jar."

"And you know I'm going to buy a couple before I leave here."

His smile sparkled in his eyes. "I'm counting on it, sugar!"

I liked Sonny, so even though I didn't like cooking, or cooking classes, or even thinking about cooking or cooking classes, I hardly broke a sweat when I gathered my courage and said, "I'm actually here about cooking classes."

"I could tell from the moment you walked in that y'all are a woman with excellent taste!" Sonny replaced the lid on the slow cooker and strode around to the front of the counter. He was dressed casually in blue jeans and a T-shirt that had pretend spatters of barbecue sauce on it along with the words *Sonny's Sauce, Sweet and Scrumptious, Y'all!* His smile still firmly in place, he looked me up and down. "I know talent when I see it. Your friend there . . ." He sized up Eve with a practiced look. "She lives on takeaway and froufrou coffee. But I figure you as a woman who knows your way around a kitchen."

I cringed. "I'm afraid you've got us mixed up. The only thing I know about my kitchen is where the phone is. I'm the one who's always calling for carryout."

He laughed. "I'll bet you make a mean chili."

"Jim does." I said it before I realized he had no idea

who I was talking about, so I added, "My fiancé. He's the cook."

"And you want to surprise him by showing him he's not the only one in the family with cookin' talent. Very smart!"

Now that I thought about it, it was a pretty good idea. Scary, but pretty good. Since I hadn't had a chance to page through the magazine I . . . ah . . . borrowed from Beth, I looked for the easy way out. "I don't suppose you have a class in making Scottish specialty foods, do you?"

"Never had a request for that one," Sonny admitted. He crossed his arms over his massive chest and settled back against the counter where the barbecue sauce was cooking. "We've got plenty of other classes, though. How about learnin' to make bread?"

"Tried it." I didn't want to elaborate. It was too embarrassing.

"Pastries?"

"If I bake them, I'll eat them. Even the ones that turn out inedible."

"Appetizers?"

That struck a chord, and I scrambled to remember everything I'd seen (and tasted) at Beth's house the Friday before. I remembered what one of the women had said about a recipe that had come from Sonny's class. "Oh, like those hokey-pokeys? That's one of your recipes, right?"

"You're darn tootin'." He bowed, taking credit. "You like?"

"They're so good!" I knew that for a fact because after I'd helped clean up the spilled champagne and broken glass, and things at the wine tasting had settled down, I'd eaten my share. "And easy to make." Which I didn't know for a fact, but it was what Beth, Glynis, and Celia had said. "That's always a good combination."

"Well, let's get the latest issue of the newsletter and see when I'm offering that class again." He started for the front of the store, greeting Eve as we passed. "I can get those by the gross," he told her, pointing to the package of toothpicks she was holding. They were candy apple red, each topped with a little cascade of shimmery streamers. Each streamer had a red heart dangling from it.

"No," I told Eve in no uncertain terms, and knowing I was investigating, she didn't argue. Or maybe it was because she never had the chance. She got distracted by a display of mint tins nearby and the sign above it that said Sonny's could personalize the tins with anything— including a picture of the happy bride and groom.

"No," I said again, but this time Eve wasn't fazed. Stars in her eyes and, no doubt, a corny picture in her head of me and Jim smiling at each other like two love-sick teenagers, she went right on looking, and I scrambled to catch up with Sonny.

"There's a summer party class coming up, too," he said as he slipped behind the front counter, and I made note of it, not because I had any intention of signing up, but because I thought something similar might work for Jim's Bellywasher's Cooking Academy. "You know, chicken wings, shish kebabs, veggies on the grill, and the like. Once the weather warms up, folks get a hankerin' for cookin' outside. They're always lookin' for something that's not burgers and dogs."

"Sounds perfect!" It did, but that wasn't what I was there about. "But I was wondering—"

"Here it is!" Sonny grabbed a copy of his monthly newsletter and pointed at the page that listed his classes.

"Appetizers So Delicious, You Might Have to Hire Somebody to Help You Enjoy Them."

Just like Sonny expected me to, I laughed at the title of the class. I also wondered if Jim shouldn't dress up his class offerings with perky names. Or maybe not. Jim was nowhere near as down-home hokey. It worked for Sonny: He had the accent and the country-boy personality to match. Jim had an accent, too, of course, but not the kind that went with corn bread and grits.

"Actually, I was wondering . . ." Sonny still had the newsletter open, and I bent nearer for a look at it. "I'd really like to take classes on Tuesday evenings. I've got the night free and—"

"Sorry, darlin'." Sonny was either a great actor or one of those rare business owners who actually cares about his customers. He looked genuinely remorseful to disappoint me. "I'm a one-man show 'cept for weekends, when the missus comes in to help out here in the store. I only teach on Saturdays."

"No. That must be wrong." My answer was automatic. So was me reaching over to pluck the newsletter out of Sonny's hands. I scanned the class list, which clearly showed that Sonny knew what he was talking about: There was a variety of classes available—all on Saturdays.

Staring at the newsletter, I raised my voice. "Eve, Sonny only teaches classes on Saturdays." I looked from the newsletter to Sonny, and I'll bet any money my expression was as incredulous as the tone of my voice. "You only teach on Saturdays."

By now, as curious as I was, Eve joined me at the front of the store. Sonny glanced from one of us to the other. "That's what I told you, ladies." Sonny lost none of his good humor in the face of what must have looked like outright looniness. "Pick a Saturday, any Saturday, and I'll be more than happy to teach you whatever cookin' technique you like. Ask about a Tuesday . . ."

"Then what about Celia, Beth, and Glynis?" Eve asked the question long before it hit her that all this was going to look crazier than ever, and confuse Sonny, to boot, so I took over.

"There are three women," I said. "Actually, there were four. Vickie, Celia, Beth, and Glynis. They told us they take cooking classes here."

"Not on Tuesday nights." Sonny was sure of this. And why shouldn't he be? It was his shop, after all. As if to prove his sincerity, he reached for a binder that sat next to the cash register. "This is my class book, where I sign folks up and mark down when they pay for classes." He paged through the binder, then nodded, confirming something to himself. "Nope. Never had women with those names in any of my classes. Not on Tuesdays or Saturdays or any other day."

"And last Saturday?" I asked, with another peek at the newsletter. "What did you teach last Saturday?"

Sonny didn't have to consult the newsletter. "A couple Saturdays ago . . ." He pointed to the entry in his newsletter. "That's when I did that hokey-pokey recipe. I'll tell you, the ladies in that class were thrilled. You know you can freeze those little suckers, then just pop them in the oven when your guests arrive." I guess we weren't as jubilant about this as he expected us to be. He went back to checking the newsletter. "The Saturday after, we did flan. Boy, the ladies sure ate that up, literally and figuratively! Last Saturday . . . see here? Last Saturday we did dips. You know, appetizers. It's a popular class because it includes my world-famous Reuben dip along with my blue cheese herb dip and pita wedges with pepperoni and provolone." He smacked his lips. "Been thinking about packaging those pita chips. The secret's in the way I keep them crispy and nobody else does it as well. You want to tell me, sugar, why my class schedule matters so much?"

Like I could actually give him an answer? Instead, all I could do was shake my head. Too bad it didn't make my thoughts settle down. Really, how could they? I'd just found out that I'd been snookered by the women who were supposed to be my newest friends.

And I'd bet both jars of barbecue sauce I was about to buy that we'd discovered something else, too.

Vickie wasn't the only one lying to her husband about where she went on Tuesday nights.

"SO, YOU'VE GOT IT ALL STRAIGHT?" I WAS AT MY desk in my office at Bellywasher's, and I turned toward the guest chair, where Eve was sitting. Once I had her attention, I propped my elbows on my knees, leaned forward, and stared at her. Hard. Years of friendship had taught me that this was usually the only way to get through to her. "You know what you're supposed to do, right?"

Eve tossed her gleaming blonde head and giggled. Years of friendship had taught me that this was usually the only way she responds when I'm trying to get through to her. "Of course I know, Annie. How hard can it be to follow one little ol' girl? Oooh!" She shivered in anticipation. "I hope that since she's not going over to Sonny's cooking school, this Celia really spends all her Tuesdays someplace like Tyson's Galleria. Wouldn't that just be the best! Being a detective and following someone, and Neiman Marcus, too!" Her sigh of utter contentment said it all. "It would be like dying and going to heaven."

Dying wasn't something I wanted to talk about.

Or even think about.

Rather than do either, I turned in the other direction to the man who stood just inside my office door. He still looked like the Jacques Lavoie I'd known for more than two years, so once in a while, I had to stop and remind myself that there's more to Jacques Lavoie, the gourmet shop owner and French chef, than meets the eye.

Which doesn't mean I love him any less.

It does mean I wanted to be really clear about what we were doing and what we were trying to accomplish. Sometimes Norman can get a little carried away. Especially when he's out in public and someone recognizes him as the Cooking Con. Norman likes the spotlight.

And apparently, a little intrigue as well. That would explain the shaggy gray wig on his head and the false mustache he had glued under his nose. It looked like a fuzzy caterpillar. The wig looked like its much bigger, much uglier cousin.

"You'll be following Glynis," I told him. "And all you need to do—"

"I know, Annie. Don't worry." Back in the day when he was pretending to be Jacques, his French accent was as thick as Pepé Le Pew's. These days, with a loyal fan following that expected him to act the part of the re- formed felon, Norman didn't try to disguise the fact that he'd spent a number of years in New Jersey. Every once in a while, a smidgen of a just-west-of-New-York-City accent crept into his voice. "Wherever she's headed, I'm on this Glynis babe like white on rice."

Like I said, sometimes Norman gets carried away.

I refused to get sidetracked by worries. Oh, it's not like I couldn't have. In a heartbeat. It was just that I knew that no matter how good a detective I was, I couldn't follow Celia, Glynis, and Beth on my own. Sure, I could take three weeks to get things sorted out, follow Beth that day, and Celia the next Tuesday, and Glynis the Tuesday after that, but I didn't want to wait that long to find out what they were up to. I refused to let Alex stay locked up in jail that long. Of course, the best of all possible scenarios was that once they left home, Celia, Glynis, and Beth would hook up. Then I could keep an eye on all three of them. If not . . . well, sometimes even Holmes had to rely on Watson. In my case, it was two Watsons. I knew I was lucky to have them, as assistants and as friends.

"You've got your cell phones?" I asked Norman and Eve, just to make sure I had all my bases covered. "We'll need to check in regularly. I want to know where everybody is at all times. I'll keep track." There was a clipboard on my desk and I lifted it for them to see. "I've made a spreadsheet, see? I'll make a note of each move Celia, Glynis, and Beth make."

"I still think walkie-talkies would be more fun." When Norman grumped, his mustache drooped over his lips. "Then we'd be like real gumshoes."

"Yeah," Eve chimed in, "like the detectives on TV."

"We're not like the detectives on TV," I reminded them both. "We're the real deal. But we've got a couple problems. We don't know where our marks are headed. And we don't want to get caught behind the eight ball. We can't take the chance that these ladies are going to ankle off and go on the lam. We don't want them to take a powder." I guess I was getting carried away, too. I shook my head to dislodge the remnants of all the old black-and-white detective movies I'd ever watched. "We know they can't be going to Sonny's on Tuesday nights. Not for cooking classes. So we need to figure out where they're really going."

"Gotcha!" With the hand that clutched the paper bearing Glynis's address, Norman gave me a crisp salute. The paper fluttered in his eyes.

"I'm ready, too," Eve said, but not before she checked her makeup and her lipstick.

I clapped my hands together. "Then let's roll."

And roll we did. Each in our own car, we headed to McLean and staked out our targets. I sat across the street from Beth and Michael's fabulous gee-whiz home, and I wasn't worried that Beth would look out a window and spot me. I didn't think she'd ever imagine that the Annie she thought was her neighbor from the big, gorgeous, expensive brick Colonial would be driving a six-year-old Saturn. But that didn't mean I was taking any chances. At six o'clock on the dot, when Beth's garage door slid open and I saw her slip behind the wheel of a black Lexus SUV, I hunkered down on the front seat just to make sure she couldn't see me. That was exactly the moment my cell phone rang.

It was Eve. I didn't bother to point out that since Celia was in one car and Eve was calling from another, she didn't have to whisper. "I'm outside Celia's house," Eve said. "She's leaving."

"So's Beth." I whispered, too. A natural response, and I told myself to cut it out.

"She's heading down the street toward the first stop sign," Eve said. "She's turning right. She's driving past a house with the prettiest rose garden. Oh, I bet it's just spectacular in the summer. She's stopping at another stop sign. She's—"

"That's terrific. Really." I couldn't take the chance of offending my Watson so I did my best to be diplomatic. "But I don't need to know every turn Celia makes."

"Oh, but you said—"

"Each move she makes. Yeah." I remembered our talk back at Bellywasher's and realized my mistake. Eve could be completely obtuse at times, and totally literal at others. The trick was that I was never sure which time was which. I scrambled to redeem myself. "What I meant is that you should call me to tell me where she ends up."

"Well, really, Annie!" Eve tsk-tsked as only Eve can. "Detective work is an analytical thing. Like a science. You need to be a little clearer when you give instructions."

"I do. I will. From now on. I promise." I was sincere, but distracted. I'd been driving three car lengths behind Beth since she left her house, and now she got on the George Washington Memorial Parkway heading east and I eased into traffic behind her. That, of course, sounds easier than it was in practice. Drivers in the D.C. metro area are notoriously competitive. If there's an inch of free space, they want it for their own. Rather than lose my concentration and risk a little too-close-for-comfort bumper-to-bumper, I told Eve we'd talk later, clamped both hands on the wheel, and kept my eyes on the road— and on Beth's SUV.

When she merged onto Arlington Boulevard, I did, too. I was glad to be off the highway when my phone rang again. It was Norman.

"We're in Arlington," he said, referring, of course, to himself and Glynis. "We're headed toward Ballston."

The call-waiting feature on my phone beeped. I switched over to the other call. It was Eve. "We're in Arlington," she said. "Near Crystal City."

And me? I wasn't all that far away from either of them.

That may sound odd, but here's the thing about Arlington: It's not a city, like most people think. Arlington is a county. In fact, since I'm a numbers sort of person, I remember from back in my high school days when I learned that, at twenty-six square miles, it's the smallest self-governing county in the country. There are no cities in the county, but there are neighborhoods, like Clarendon, where Très Bonne Cuisine is located, and Ballston, where Glynis was headed, and Crystal City, which was apparently Celia's destination.

As for Beth, she was driving in the direction of Rosslyn, the area just north of Arlington National Cemetery. With the way traffic was moving faster than the posted speed limit and drivers doing their best to outpace each other, I really had to concentrate to keep an eye on her SUV. Up ahead, she slowed down and I did, too. The car behind her turned left. So did the car behind that one. Like it or not, at the next red light, I found myself right behind her.

I wasn't about to take any chances, not after getting this far. I slunk down in my seat and propped one elbow on the steering wheel so I could use my hand to partially cover my face. "I'm in Arlington, too," I told Eve, keeping my voice down in spite of the fact that I knew I didn't have to. "This is just weird."

"Do you suppose they're all going to meet somewhere?" she asked.

And honestly, I couldn't say. The light turned green and we started up again, and when a pushy driver wedged his pricey sports car between Beth's SUV and my sensible sedan, I was grateful. I eased back a bit, but I never took my eyes off Beth's car.

A couple quick turns and I saw her brake lights flash on. She turned into the parking lot of a place called Preston's Colonial House. I still had my cell phone to my ear, and I was about to report this turn of events to Eve when she said, "Fergie's."

"Huh?" I couldn't follow Beth into the parking lot without her seeing me, so I hung back, pretending I was waiting for a parking place to open up on the street. "What do you mean, Fergie's? Beth just went into—"

"Celia just walked into a place called Fergie's," Eve reported. "It looks nice. Upscale. Well-dressed people coming and going. It's a bar."

"So's the Colonial House." I didn't have time to consider what this meant. My phone beeped and Norman got on the line with his report.

"The Purple Tiger," he said. "It's a bar. Looks like a younger crowd. Hip and trendy. You know the type."

I didn't want to burst his bubble and tell him I wouldn't know hip and trendy if it walked up and introduced itself. Instead, I got lucky and a parking place on the street opened up. I slid the Saturn into it, then grabbed my clipboard and took notes.

Under the column that said *Celia* in bold, black letters, I wrote *Fergie's in Crystal City* along with the time. I did the same for Beth and Glynis, listing the names of the bars they'd gone to, the time they entered, and—

"Now we wait," I told Norman, though since I heard his car door slam, I didn't think he was listening.

"No worries," he said, sounding as carefree as he did on his TV show when he was combining what sounded like impossible-to-go-together ingredients into what always turned out to be an incredible meal. "She doesn't know me. It's perfect, Annie. I can keep an eye on Glynis. You know, up close and personal."

"Not too up close and personal," I warned him, at the same time I clicked back over to Eve. "Not too—," I'd just said when I heard her car door slam, too.

That left me, and I couldn't go inside, because Beth would recognize me in an instant. I groaned and reminded myself that even one Holmes couldn't follow three suspicious characters. I was lucky to have my Watsons, and I'd be luckier still if they didn't get spotted and blow the operation.

As for me, I snapped my cell phone shut, pulled the clipboard onto my lap, and waited to see when Beth would come out of Preston's.

I did something else, too.

I wondered why each of these women had gone into a different bar, what were they doing there, and what it all had to do with Vickie's murder.

Ten

BY THE FOLLOWING FRIDAY, I STILL DIDN'T HAVE THE answers to my questions, but I knew where I had to look to find them. I would, too. As soon as I got over the shock and awe of getting my first up-close-and-personal gander at Celia's house.

Beth's home was a modern wonder of sleek lines and serene colors. Celia's was anything but. No stylish angles or two-story panes of glass here. With its hand-hewn stone walls, its slate roof, and the little half-circle windows that peeked from gables, Celia and Scott's house looked as if it had been plucked from the English countryside. In fact, the only thing it had in common with Beth and Michael's palatial home was the too cute *Welcome Friends* sign near the front door. Yeah, the one with the smiling, waving bear and moose on it.

Bear and moose aside, I tried not to look too impressed when I stepped through a charming swinging gate that led up an equally charming stone walk lined with an array of early blooming (and not incidently, very charming) wildflowers.

I actually might have been caught in the fairy-tale wonder of it all if the door didn't open even before I rang the bell.

And if Edward Monroe wasn't standing there.

Before I could make a move, he stepped outside and closed the door behind him. "I heard you'd be here," he said. He looked beyond me to Norman's Jag parked on the other side of the street. "I'm surprised you didn't walk. It's such a beautiful evening."

"I was running late. And with so much to carry . . ." I had a tote bag with me, and I hoisted it in both hands just to demonstrate. "I hope Celia isn't waiting for me before she puts the food out. I wouldn't want to hold up the festivities."

Edward's expression never changed. "Oh, the girls are a little busy," he said. "Beth's in a real tizzy. You know how she can get."

I didn't, since I didn't know Beth well enough to know if she was tizzy-prone. I nodded like I did, anyway. "She's upset? About . . . ?"

Edward didn't answer. In fact, all he did was stare. So hard and so long, it made me uncomfortable. I shifted my tote bag from my right hand to my left, then back to my right. "If there's anything I can do to help . . ." I finally said, making a move toward the door.

Edward blocked my path. "I suppose the only thing anybody can do to help is to find that money for her."

I was pretty sure my blank expression was all the response Edward would need. But he apparently was not so convinced. He cocked his head and raised his voice just enough to make it clear that perhaps I hadn't heard him right the first time, and if only I'd listen a little closer, maybe I'd get things straight. "The Girl Scout cookie money," he said, slowly, each word pronounced distinctly. "There's five hundred dollars of Girl Scout cookie money missing and Beth's worried sick about it. She doesn't want Michael to find out, so don't say a thing once you're inside. She probably wouldn't have mentioned it to me except . . . well . . ." He twitched his shoulders as if the thought made him uncomfortable. "She apparently thought I could help her out, though how I can, I'm not sure. But then, maybe she's not thinking straight. She's terribly upset."

"I can certainly understand that." My own stomach did flip-flops at the very thought, and it wasn't even my cookie money. "Maybe she's just misplaced it. That kind of thing happens a lot. We put something down in one place, and we're convinced we put it someplace else. We make ourselves sick with worry when all we have to do is stop and think things through."

"Maybe." Edward wasn't convinced. I could tell because he crossed his arms over his chest.

I managed a smile. "Maybe she needs to re-create the incident. You know, go over the details in her head. When was the last time she saw the money?"

"She says it was at her house. Last Friday. You know, the day you came over for the wine tasting."

Yes, of course I knew that. I didn't point it out. "And where was the last place she saw it?"

Edward's eagle-eyed gaze never wavered. "She thinks it was in the kitchen. There's a desk in there where she and Michael take care of bills and such. She's sure that's where she left the envelope with the money in it. You may have seen it, Annie. You were in the kitchen. Alone."

OK, call me slow. Call me dense, to boot. It took a

while for what he was saying to sink it, and even after it had, I was pretty sure I was imagining things.

I swallowed hard. "You're not saying—"

His eyes opened wide in feigned surprise, Edward took a step back. "I'd never accuse anyone of something like that. Not until I had some proof, anyway."

That was a relief. I reminded myself that suspicious looks and veiled accusations weren't enough proof for anyone and reached around Edward to press the front bell. Pretending I'd just arrived was the perfect excuse for me to get away from him. "Maybe I can help Beth figure out what happened," I said, a smile on my face. "I'm pretty good when it comes to getting down to the bottom of mysteries."

I don't know how he might have responded, because Celia showed up at the oak door, which was twice as tall as me, and led me into a foyer complete with a suit of armor, ancestral pictures on the walls (they didn't look like the forebears of either Celia or Scott), and a flagstone floor that I had no doubt was a pain to keep clean.

In a lightweight tweedy sweater and neatly tailored pants, Celia fit right in. She looked like the lady of the manor.

In my black pants and one of the spring tops I'd bought back when I worked at the bank, I looked like exactly what I was: a poser.

Fortunately, no one seemed to hold it against me. Glynis and Beth came out of the kitchen to greet me, as friendly as ever in spite of the cookie money drama, and eager to make me feel right at home. I might have relaxed if I didn't look back into the foyer just in time to see Edward walk back in.

I stopped for a moment and studied him as closely as he was looking at me.

I thought Edward Monroe was a murderer, and that gave me every right to be suspicious, right? But suspicious or not, I wasn't prepared for what had just happened.

Because I'd just found out that Edward was suspicious, too. There was money missing from Beth's. And without coming right out and saying it, Edward had delivered a clear message:

He thought I was the one who'd taken it.

FORTUNATELY, MY NEWEST BEST FRIENDS APPARently either hadn't heard Edward's take on the missing money or didn't buy into it. I followed them into the kitchen and, back in my element (No, not that element! Not the kitchen, investigating!), I knew I had the upper hand. Ever since the previous Tuesday, when Norman, Eve, and I did our James Bond thing and found out that there was more to these ladies than I'd imagined, I'd been planning for this meeting. I was as pleased as punch to see that the evening was materializing into exactly the showdown I was hoping for. I stood back, watched, and waited as Celia pulled a heart-shaped red porcelain casserole dish out of the oven.

"Reuben dip." She beamed. "Scott loves Reubens and this is easier than making sandwiches. And you know, they say the recipe from Sonny's cooking school is the best ever." She set the cast-iron casserole on the granite island in the center of the kitchen, where Glynis was arranging her appetizer on a glorious Waterford crystal serving tray.

"Pita wedges," Glynis said. "They're topped with pepperoni and slices of provolone, and only Sonny knows the secret of how to keep them crispy, even though there's olive oil and butter, too, in the recipe." She giggled. "Sonny only shares his secrets with his students."

All the while, Beth fiddled with a ceramic platter shaped like an octagon and decorated in a berry pattern. I'd seen the same platter on sale at Très Bonne Cuisine for more than two hundred bucks. I'd seen porcelain cookware like Celia's, too, and I knew it cost a pretty penny, even on special. I'd never seen the Waterford on sale anywhere. But then, Target doesn't have a Waterford department.

"Blue cheese herb dip," Beth said, smiling down at the concoction as if it were a favorite child. "It's one of Sonny's specialties."

Celia stepped back and looked over the arrangement of serving dishes, gleaming silver, and sprucely pressed linen napkins. "Perfect," she said with a satisfied sigh. "And what did you bring, Annie? We'll make room for whatever it is."

I thought she'd never ask.

I reached inside the tote bag I was carrying and, one by one, drew out my contributions to the night's festivities. I'd brought three items, each in the little plastic grocery store container I'd bought it in.

I popped open the first container. "Reuben dip," I said, setting it down next to Celia's creation. "We might want to heat it in the microwave eventually. But we should probably wait until yours is all gone. No use having two of them going at the same time."

Apparently oblivious to the stifled gasps behind me, I stripped the plastic band from around the cover of the second container and plunked it on the island next to Glynis's gleaming crystal dish. "Pita wedges," I said. "I tried a sample over at Whole Foods and they may not be as crispy as Sonny's, but they're really good." I was sure to keep my smile firmly in place when I delivered the pièce de résistance along with my last appetizer. "Blue cheese herb dip," I said, taking the plastic lid off the container. "It might not be as good as Sonny's but . . ." I looked from one woman to the other. "Anyone care for a sample?"

Just as I expected, my offer—and my offerings—were met with open-mouthed wonder.

"How did you . . ." Celia stuttered.

"How could you . . ." Glynis stammered.

Beth didn't do anything but drop her jaw and snap it shut again. Like a fish that had been hooked and dragged out of the water.

And me? Satisfied that I'd gotten the reaction I expected, I crossed my arms over my chest. "Anyone want to explain? Or would you like me to start throwing out theories and we'll see which one sticks?" I gave each of them a measured look.

Beth turned as pale as a ghost.

Color shot into Glynis's cheeks.

With one hand, Celia clutched the corner of the island so hard, her knuckles turned white.

She shot a look over her shoulder toward the great room, where we could hear the men chatting. "We can't talk," she said. "Not here."

"Then where?"

"We could talk . . ." Beth looked toward the great room, too. Inside her jumper decorated with cute embroidered teddy bears, her chest heaved. "Another time, maybe."

Glynis jumped right in. "Another place. You could bring the girls to the playground tomorrow and—"

I stopped them with a no-nonsense shake of my head. "Here," I said. "Now."

Celia swallowed hard. She nodded. "Now. But not here." She grabbed my arm and dragged me toward the sliding doors that led outside and all four of us stumbled out onto a flagstone patio where a fuzzy layer of moss grew between each paver, as pretty as a picture. We made our way around a thick border of hyacinths and tulips and past a trickling fountain and an outdoor fireplace, and we finally pushed through another gate, the twin of the one out front. Ahead of us was another acre or so of flagstones and at the center of it, a swimming pool as big as the one at my old high school. We stopped there, but not for long. One glance and I knew why. The great room also overlooked the swimming pool and the patio.

As one, each of the women waved to her husband.

As one, each of them waved back. All except Edward Monroe. One by one, he looked us over. His gaze rested on me longer than it did on the others. His hand tightened around the stem of his wineglass.

I had the feeling he was about to step out of the French doors, point a finger, and announce to the world that I was the biggest thief since Jean Valjean. Before he could make his move, Celia tightened her hold and dragged me to the other side of the pool.

When we got there, I shook out of her grasp. "I don't think they'll hear us here," I said, but Celia didn't look so sure. One more look around and she caught hold of my arm again and pulled me to a freestanding little building surrounded by shrubs and an edging of daffodils. There was a combination lock on the door, and she quickly spun through the numbers until it snapped open.

"We're having trouble with the sauna," she mumbled, setting the lock down on a nearby rock. "We don't want the kids messing with it. In here." She opened the door and nudged me through it. As soon as Beth and Glynis were inside, too, Celia closed the door. "If Scott asks," she said, "I'll tell him you're thinking of installing a sauna and you wanted a tour. Unless you have a sauna?"

"No sauna." It was as truthful as I was ever likely to be. I not only didn't own a sauna, I'd never been inside one. While the women paced, ordering their thoughts and (I had no doubt) trying to decide how much I knew, how I knew it, and how much they were willing to confess about their cooking skills—or lack of them—I took a quick look around.

The sauna consisted of a single room. It was large and comfortable, made entirely of cedar, and with U-shaped seating large enough for . . . I did a quick tally. The way I saw it, at least twelve people could comfortably occupy the sauna at any one time. Across from the benches built into the wall was a heater. I stationed myself right in front of it, and, realizing I wasn't going to let them off the hook, one by one, the women took their seats.

Without any introduction, I launched into what I'd been planning to tell them since the Tuesday before, when I found myself outside Preston's Colonial House watching Beth go inside. "I bought all my appetizers at the grocery store. The same place you all bought yours."

Glynis half rose. "But Sonny—"

I stopped her with one pointed look. "I'm not dissing Sonny. Believe me, I'm sure he makes all the things in his classes that he says he makes in his classes. But, see, I finally figured out why you were so happy when you found out I took cooking classes at Très Bonne Cuisine. You knew a cooking friend would come in handy someday. And I did, the day Michael wanted fresh-baked flan and none of you were able to make it for him. You see, besides realizing once and for all that I never want to attempt flan again, there's another thing I figured out. I know you don't attend any of Sonny's cooking classes. You see, Sonny's cooking classes are only held on Saturdays."

"Is that what this is all about?" Celia practically sounded cocky. Her mouth thinned. "All you had to do is ask, Annie. We're special." She looked at her friends and managed a giggle that might have been convincing if I hadn't known she was lying through her teeth. "Sonny gives us private lessons on Tuesdays."

"Really? You're not in any of his class books," I said, and I watched the starch go right out of Celia's shoulders. "You've never been in any of his class books, because you've never been in any of Sonny's classes. He's never heard of you. Any of you."

"How would you know?" This from Glynis, whose bland eyes practically snapped with annoyance. "And what difference does it make, anyway? Why do you care where we get our recipes?"

Even though I was in full control of the situation, I couldn't help but gulp with trepidation. Talk of cooking always does that to me. As if to prove how unconcerned I was, I held up both hands and took a step back. "Recipes? I don't care. I've never cared. Believe me! When it comes to cooking, there's no way on earth I could care less. And I wouldn't care now. If it wasn't for Vickie."

Beth stifled a tiny sob, but then, she apparently didn't have nearly the gumption of her two friends. Celia and Glynis rose from their seats.

"Vickie?" Celia was shorter than me. When she looked up at me, her top lip curled. "You didn't even know Vickie. You don't care. And telling people we take cooking classes from Sonny, that has nothing to do with Vickie."

I kept my voice even, the better to try to lull them into complacency. "Sure it does. Because Vickie said she was going to cooking classes, too. Fact is, she was going to Swallows every Tuesday night instead. Another fact is, when the cops asked you about it, you said Vickie always had an excuse. You told the police that on one Tuesday, Vickie said she had a headache and couldn't make it to class. On another, you told the cops, Vickie said both her kids were sick and she had to stay home with them. A third fact . . ." I cut to the chase. "What you never bothered to mention was that if there was a cooking class and if Vickie was in it, you never would have known, anyway. None of you. Because you were—you are—doing exactly what Vickie was doing every Tuesday night. You're all going out on the town."

Celia dropped back down on the bench.

Glynis sputtered.

Beth slapped one hand to her open mouth. Her eyes got big. Her face turned as white as the eyeballs of the teddy bears on her jumper. When she managed to choke out a few words, her voice was nearly lost beneath another sob. "Oh, my God, you're a cop!"

I swear, I almost laughed. And maybe that would have been a good thing. Maybe it would have helped relieve some of the tension that built in the room like the heat must have done when the sauna was working.

I knew I'd lose my advantage if I was too easy on them, so I kept my expression blank and my voice firm. "I'm not a cop." My inherently honest nature kicked in big time. I knew it would eventually. "I'm a private detective."

"And you think we killed Vickie!" Where she got that

idea, I didn't know, but Beth was so convinced, tears welled in her eyes. "Oh, I knew this was going to happen. I told you." She jumped off the bench so she could face her two friends. "I told you we'd get in trouble if we did what we were doing. But you wouldn't listen."

Celia tossed her head. Her inky hair moved like silk. "Nobody was in trouble. Not until Vickie decided to go back to the same place, over and over again. Not until she decided—"

Beth folded her arms over her chest. The teddy bears on her jumper peeked out over her forearms. "She didn't decide anything. It just happened."

Glynis stuck out her lower lip. "That's not what we were there for," she told Beth.

Beth's glare was monumental. "Oh, yeah? Then what were we there for?"

Celia hopped back up on her feet. "It was supposed to just be fun. Maybe you forgot that."

"Maybe you"—Beth pointed a finger at Celia's nose— "maybe you forgot that feelings can't be turned off and on like the switch on the side of your cappuccino maker. You can't recognize that you have feelings for somebody, then just walk away. Vickie knew that. Vickie was honest and trusting."

"Yeah." Celia sneered. "And look where it got her."

"At least she took a chance," Beth sniffed and said. "At least she wasn't afraid, not like you two."

"Afraid?" It was Glynis's turn to be outraged. "If Vickie had listened to us in the first place—"

"But she didn't listen. She couldn't listen," Beth insisted. "She was too busy listening to her heart!"

"Oh, please!" Celia managed to turn the phrase into three syllables. "You must be reading too many corny greeting cards."

Beth threw back her shoulders. "And you must be completely out of your mind. But then, you've always been a little ditzy."

"Oh, yeah?" Celia screamed. It wasn't a great comeback, but it must have been good enough because Beth echoed it with her own, "Oh, yeah."

And I knew I had to do something—fast—before an ugly situation got even worse.

"Ladies!" I stepped between Beth and Celia. It got them to back off, but it didn't do a thing to soften the glares they shot in each other's direction. I kept my voice soft and even. Like I tried so hard to do when dealing with Fi's kids. "This isn't what I intended to happen," I said, as truthful as can be. "I don't want to see you guys fight. I'm just looking to find out what really happened to Vickie."

"Vickie was stupid." Celia dropped back down on the cedar bench.

"Vickie forgot that there were rules." Glynis took a seat beside her.

That left Beth, and I turned to her. I wasn't sure why she was defending Vickie when the other women weren't, but right about then, I didn't care. I needed answers. I looked her in the eye. "I think there's a lot for us to talk about. How about if you sit down, too?"

She did. But she made sure she kept her distance from the other two women.

Back in control—but who knew for how long?—I started again. "Look, there doesn't seem to be any point in lying to you any longer—"

"Yeah." Glynis glowered. "Now that we know you're a private investigator."

"That's not why." I hunkered down, the better to look each of the women in the eye. At the same time, I put my left hand on Celia's arm (she was farthest in that direction) and my right on Beth's. "I want you to know the truth because I think . . . well, I like to think of you as my friends. Even though you did con me into making that flan for you. And I can understand if you don't feel very friendly toward me any longer. After all, I did lie to you. But that's the whole point of friendship, isn't it? We can have differences, and we can talk them out. Right?"

One by one, they nodded their begrudging agreement.

"Then here's what you have to know." I cleared my throat and, because I wasn't in the kind of shape that allowed me to sit in a catcher's squat for any length of time and still be able to walk, I stood and tried not to wince when my thigh muscles screamed in protest. "Alex Bannerman, the guy who's accused of killing Vickie . . . Alex is a friend of mine. I'm looking into Vickie's murder because I'm trying to clear Alex's name."

Celia's protest was immediate. "We can't help you."

"You can." I couldn't afford to single any of them out, so I took in all three women with a wave of one arm. "You can tell me what you're up to on Tuesday nights."

"But if we do—"

Celia and Glynis both shushed Beth with a look.

"If you don't, Alex is going to end up in prison for a crime he didn't commit," I reminded them.

Glynis looked up at the ceiling. "The cops say he did it."

Celia looked down at the floor. "The papers say the evidence is indisputable."

Beth wiped a finger under nose. "The TV news says there's no doubt."

"And none of them are right." I kept the desperation from my voice. Barely. "Alex is a nice guy. A really nice guy. He's fun, and he's funny. He makes really great cookies, only he calls them biscuits. He's remodeling the house where I'm going to live."

"And let me guess . . . that isn't here in McLean, is it?" The pointed question came from Celia along with a look that matched.

"It isn't," I admitted. "The part about me being one of your new neighbors was a lie, too. I needed to get to know you so I could find out more about Vickie. I didn't think you'd give me the time of day, not if you didn't think I was one of you."

Glynis sighed.

Celia picked at one leg of her tailored pants.

Beth cried softly.

I thought she'd be the first to cave, but, surprisingly, the surrender came from Celia. "Look . . ." She shifted her position on the bench. "This isn't something we want anyone to find out about. The guys—"

"They think we go to cooking class every Tuesday night," Glynis added.

"Which is why you check Sonny's schedule to see what he's making in his classes. Then you do exactly what I did, right? You check out the ready-made foods at the grocery stores, find something similar, buy it, and make it look homemade by heating it in a fancy porcelain pan or scooping it out of its little plastic container and serving it on crystal."

"Guilty." Glynis tried for a smile that didn't exactly make it all the way to her eyes. "We've been doing it for just about a year now."

"And on Tuesdays, when your husbands think you're going to cooking class, you've been going to bars, and I don't get it. Unless . . ." OK, call me slow. A lightbulb went off in my head and suddenly the whole thing made sense. It was a sick and twisted sense, but it was sense nonetheless. "You're all doing exactly what Vickie was doing. You go out on Tuesday nights to meet guys."

Not a single one of them jumped up and told me I was wrong. They didn't have to. I knew from the color in Glynis's cheeks and the paleness of Celia's and the way Beth twitched her nose . . . I knew I was right.

"Well, what do you expect?" Celia harrumphed the explanation. "You don't really think it's easy to be perfect, do you?"

It was my turn to be speechless. Which was why Glynis had a chance to interject, "Life in the 'burbs isn't all it's cracked up to be. We've got to be perfect wives."

"And perfect mothers," Beth added.

Celia joined the bandwagon. "We've got to have perfect clothes and perfect wardrobes and perfect manners."

"Perfect meals, perfect taste, perfect children." Glynis looked perfectly miserable about the whole thing. "It's impossible."

"Who can blame us for wanting to step out now and again?" Celia asked.

I didn't get it. But I wasn't about to argue. "So every Tuesday . . . ?"

"Every Tuesday, we each head out to have a little fun." Celia glanced at her two friends. "The rules have always been the same. We're never supposed to go to the same bar twice."

"And we're always supposed to say we're going to cooking class," Glynis added.

"We're not supposed to talk about what happens while we're out," Celia said.

"Not even to each other."

I grumbled under my breath. "But then, that means—"

"That we really don't know who Vickie was seeing or what she was up to," Glynis finished my sentence for me.

"She did say she'd met someone." Beth's voice was so low, we all leaned forward to hear her. "Someone special."

"She told you that?" Celia wasn't as surprised as she was obviously pissed that she'd been left out of the loop.

Beth shrugged. "She mentioned it. That's all. She never gave me the details. She just said . . . you know. She just said he was special."

I swallowed hard. "Do you think she was talking about Alex?"

Beth answered with another shrug.

It was my turn to drop down on the bench. "Then none of this helps us much, does it? Vickie was probably talking about Alex. We know they saw each other every week at Swallows, so we know she ignored the rule about going to the same bar twice. But that doesn't mean he killed her," I added, just so they didn't get the wrong impression. "Alex didn't know she was married. And he really liked Vickie. And—"

I listened to my own words and realized I was right back where I started from. "I'm sorry I lied," I said, and I meant it. "Maybe we could have gotten this whole thing straightened out right from the beginning if I'd just told you the truth from day one. But I wanted to get to know all of you and . . ." I didn't dare say what I was thinking. I hardly dared admit it to myself.

I wanted these women's lives. I liked pretending I was a suburban wife and mother who had all the material comforts a restaurant manager could only dream of. Celia, Glynis, and Beth were living my dream life. Or at least what I'd always thought my dream life was.

Finding out that even the most perfect lives weren't all that perfect was a hard dose to swallow.

For all of us.

"Look," I said, "I know there's no reason you should listen to my advice, but I do have some experience when it comes to this kind of thing. That lie about you going to cooking classes on Tuesday nights is going to come back to bite you. You know that, don't you? You really should come clean with your husbands." I thought about Jim, about the kind of honest, authentic relationship we had with each other. It was something I wanted to last forever. It was hard for me to get my brain around the idea of couples who didn't have—or didn't want—that kind of intimacy. I guess I was talking to myself as much as to the other women when I said, "Isn't being open and honest with each other what marriage is all about?"

Celia rolled her eyes. "You're not really married, are you?" she asked before she got up and headed out the door.

Glynis followed her.

Beth dragged behind. I got the feeling there was more she wanted to say, but when I gave her the opportunity by asking, "Is something bothering you?" she just hurried outside.

And me? Well, I should have been thinking about my case, but let's face it, though I'd satisfied my curiosity about what the women did on Tuesday nights, I really hadn't learned much that was going to help me find Vickie's killer, had I?

Maybe that was why I didn't want to think about it. Maybe it was just too depressing to realize that I was no closer to clearing Alex's name than I had been before we walked inside the sauna.

Or maybe I was just too preoccupied with everything Celia, Glynis, and Beth had revealed. And everything they didn't need to say: all that stuff about marriage and how maybe reality could never live up to my fantasies.

Maybe my pie-in-the-sky version of how things were going to be for Jim and me would never actually mesh, not in real life.

Maybe I should have learned that from my marriage to Peter.

I sat there for a few minutes, deep in thought, before I shook myself back to reality.

"Snap out of it, Annie," I reminded myself and headed for the door. "You're not Celia, Glynis, Beth, or Vickie. And Jim isn't a thing like any of their husbands. He's certainly nothing like Peter. Jim and I will always be honest with each other. We'll always be open—"

As fate would have it, that was the exact moment I pushed on the door. Only the door never moved.

"Open," I said again, and gave it another push.

But the door didn't budge.

To say I was surprised was an understatement, and, thinking about it, I stepped back and considered my options. That was just about the same time I heard the heat in the sauna click on.

Eleven

✂

SO WHO CAN BLAME ME? I STOOD THERE FOR A FEW dumbstruck moments, the panic closing in while the heat rose, not little by little, the way I imagine it's supposed to in a sauna, but by leaps and bounds. What had Celia said? The sauna was acting up? Oh, yeah. Big time. Even little ol' unmechanical me knew that. Even before I shook off the surprise and fear that kept me rooted to the spot, there was a thin stream of perspiration on my forehead and another one on my upper lip.

I flicked it aside and shook myself out of my daze. "It's a machine, Annie," I reminded myself. "And machines can be controlled. You're not stuck in some suburban house of horrors."

Keeping the thought in mind, I tamped back my fear and did my best to approach this problem like I did everything else: logically, reasonably, carefully.

There were control buttons on the side of the sauna heater unit, and I fiddled with them, stepped back, and waited for the promise of cooler air.

No dice.

In fact, I swear the temperature climbed another few degrees.

"Logically, reasonably, carefully," I told myself. "Logically, reasonably, carefully." The mantra might actually have helped if I didn't suddenly feel like a Thanksgiving turkey that had been shoved in the oven and left to baste in its own juices. I lifted the hem of my top and flapped it to cool myself off, and the strategy worked, at least for a few seconds. Before I could heat up again, I went back to the door. When it didn't open, I pounded on it with my fists, and when no one answered, I cursed myself for keeping my cell phone in my purse and my purse in Celia's kitchen. I looked around, considering my options.

They were limited, but not nonexistent.

"Logically, reasonably, carefully," I told myself, climbing up on one of the cedar benches against the wall. If I could reach the skylight on the ceiling . . .

Yeah, I don't know what I intended to accomplish, either, but I thought maybe the skylight up there might open. Seeing that I was a couple feet too short to get anywhere near finding out, it didn't really matter. I hopped back to the floor and sat down, hauling in breath after stifling breath. How long I sat there, I don't know. I may have drifted off for a few minutes. I do know that by the time I snapped myself out of the daze, I was drained and weak, and my head was swimming. One glance at my clothes and I realized I looked like I'd been swimming, too. My shirt stuck to my body and a stream of perspiration trickled between my breasts. My pants were soaked and clung to my legs like wet rags. My hair was too curly even on the best days and with the added oomph of the heat, I could practically hear it springing into wild curlicues all over my head.

And none of it mattered. At least not as much as getting out of that sauna alive.

"Logically, reasonably . . ." I tried to comfort myself with the mantra again, but I couldn't remember the rest of it. The words floated out of my head, just like I felt I was floating above the cedar floorboards. I made myself take another stab at it. "Logically . . ." I said, but the rest of the phrase failed me. I rubbed my knuckles across my eyes and pressed them to my temples. My head pounded. So did my heart.

"Logibally, reasonically . . ." Was that my voice? It was so strained and muffled, it sounded like it came from a million miles away. "Carebally," I told myself. "When you're investigabating a murderous murder, you've got to be reasonically logical."

So reasonically logical I was.

At least that's what I thought at the time.

I plucked the thermometer off the wall and without even looking to see how high the temperature was, I flung the thermometer at the skylight. I missed by a mile and on the way down, the thermometer clunked me in the head.

I picked up the huge, shallow spoon that's used to toss water onto the hot sauna coals and tried to crack the skylight with that, too, and had no better luck. When the ladle landed on the floor next to me, I picked it up and hurled it at the door.

Good thing I'm a bad pitcher and the ladle hit the wall instead of the door. Just at that moment, the door opened and Celia stuck her head inside the sauna.

"Annie?" She took one look at me and hurried inside, but not before she propped the discarded ladle against the door. A wave of wonderful, fresh, cool air streamed into the sauna. My clothes were so damp, I shivered.

"Annie?" Celia grabbed my shoulders and gave me a little shake. "We wondered where you were and what happened and—"

"I was being logiable," I told her. "But I couldn't get out."

She looked over her shoulder at the door and I was just not-out-of-it enough to know something was wrong.

"I told you the sauna wasn't working right. There's no way it should be able to be turned on from anywhere but right in here. But somebody must have done that. And put the lock back on the door after Glynis, Beth, and I left." I was the one who was woozy, but Celia swayed on her feet. But if they knew you were in here, nobody ever would have done that. Unless . . . Unless . . ." I wasn't seeing straight, but I saw that Celia's complexion turned green. "My goodness, Annie, I know this is going to sound crazy, but it looks like somebody tried to kill you."

I DON'T KNOW ABOUT THAT. I MEAN, SURE, PEOPLE had tried to kill me before. Any number of times. I'd had the brake lines on my car cut. There had once been a doctor who wanted to keep me quiet, and she tried to shoot air into my veins through an IV line. And just recently, Eve and I had been kidnapped by a man who threatened us with a knife. Sometimes I still had bad dreams about that big, shiny knife and the crazy man wielding it.

But really, if somebody wanted me dead, there seemed to be plenty of better ways of doing it. Roasting me alive didn't strike me as either efficient or decisive.

Then again, it definitely sent a message, and a troubling one at that. Is that what someone was trying to do? Was that someone Edward Monroe? And how far was he willing to go to prove a point?

Thinking through the problem, was I sounding logical and reasonable again? Finally!

That was thanks to the fact that after Celia dragged me out of the sauna, she took me into the house and made me drink a couple gallons of water. Then she poured a tepid bath for me (the tub in the master suite was almost as big as the pool outside) and when I was done soaking, she, Glynis, and Beth fluttered around me like mother hens taking care of a favorite chick.

"This is so awful." We were back in the kitchen and Celia apparently decided that I needed to replace all the salt that had been sweated out of my system. She shoved a plate at me heaped with Reuben dip and Triscuits. "Somebody must have assumed we'd all left the sauna. That's why the lock was back on the door." The three women weren't the only ones gathered around me. The men were there, too, all except for Edward Monroe, I noticed, who was suspiciously absent.

Celia glanced around at the guys, who all shook their heads, denying any accountability for the sauna fiasco. Her dark eyes flashed. "Well, I'm going to have a talk with the kids, that's for sure. If one of them pulled that stunt, they're going to be grounded until they're out of college."

Beth brought me a glass of lemonade. "Are you sure you feel OK?" She looked to Michael for guidance. "Maybe we should call EMS after all?"

I couldn't say no, because my mouth was full of crackers and dip. I shook my head instead. After I swallowed, I said, "I'm fine. Really. Even if one of the kids did it . . ." I doubted this was true, but going along with the story might get me information and, at a time like this, information was what I needed. "You know it was an accident. You've all been so kind taking care of me. And I feel much better. Really."

"No headache?" I don't know how she thought it would prove it, but Celia pressed the back of one hand to my forehead. "No nausea? No chills?"

My mouth was full again so again, I shook my head. Celia had given me one of her bathrobes to wear while my clothes were in the washer and dryer and I didn't want to move too fast. Celia is short and dainty. I am short and anything but. I wouldn't have been so self-conscious if the guys weren't gathered around. I set down my plate and cinched the belt on the robe so I could stand. It was a relief to realize my knees weren't rubbery anymore. "I think I'll just head home," I said. "I mean, after I get dressed."

That seemed to be enough to satisfy the men. Nodding the way people do when a crisis has been handled and all is well again, they grabbed their wineglasses and went back to the great room.

I watched them go and pretended I'd just noticed. "Edward isn't here any longer."

Beth's mouth thinned in a way that told me I'd hit a nerve, but she didn't say a word.

"He's taking Henry and Antonia to their grandmother's for the night." Glynis supplied the explanation. "He was gone even before we realized you were missing."

"Is that true, Beth?" I turned to her. "You look as if you're not quite sure."

"Of course I'm sure. And what difference would it make, anyway?"

It wouldn't have, if Beth didn't look so darned jumpy. She bustled around the kitchen, straightening and refilling the serving dishes even though none of them needed it.

I closed in on her and pretended to be reaching for some of her blue cheese herb dip so I could lay one of my hands on hers to still her. I kept my voice low so Celia and Glynis—on the other side of the kitchen choosing a bottle of wine out of the wine chiller built in near the pantry—wouldn't hear. "You want to talk?"

Beth glanced up only long enough to make sure her friends weren't watching. She nodded.

I knew I had to act fast, before she changed her mind. "Come on, Beth," I said, backing off from the island and the food that looked better than ever now that I was feeling more like myself. "You can show me where my laundry is."

The basement of Celia's house was far more elegant than my apartment. There was a cheery finished room with a wall of shelves for toys, a bunch of those low-slung rocking video chairs, and a huge flat-panel TV. There was another room Celia used exclusively for her scrapbooking. The lighting was so good in there, it could have doubled as an operating room. Beyond that was the laundry room. The dryer buzzed just as we walked in.

I retrieved my clothes and stepped into a little side room where the shelves along one wall were stacked with extra bottles of laundry detergent and fabric softener.

"So . . ." Since Beth politely stayed out by the washer and dryer, I raised my voice so she could hear me and slipped into my underwear. "I can't help but feel there's something you want to tell me, Beth." Just to make sure she was listening, I stuck my head out the door. Beth had her back against the washing machine. She was wringing her hands and there were tears running down her cheeks. I stepped into my pants and pulled my top over my head. Barefoot—I had no idea what had happened to my black flats—I walked out of the storage room.

"Does this have anything to do with the missing Girl Scout cookie money?" I asked.

I think she actually might have laughed if she wasn't so totally miserable. Beth shook her head. "The cookie money . . . I mean, it's incredibly embarrassing to have to admit you misplaced five hundred dollars. I can't let Michael find out. He'd be so upset and embarrassed. I mean, especially with the new promotion and him being in charge of millions of dollars at the company. If word went around that I couldn't even keep five hundred dollars straight . . ." She shivered at the thought. "This whole thing about the cookie money is the straw that broke that camel's back, Annie. I'm so stressed, so worried. But the cookie money, it's nothing compared to—" She paused and looked up at the ceiling.

And I knew I had to nudge her, just a little, or she'd get stuck in her uncertainty. I took a step nearer. "When I asked about Edward leaving early this evening, you looked a little upset."

Beth chewed on her lower lip.

"If there's something you know—"

Her sob stopped me. Beth brushed both her hands over her cheeks. She sniffled. "I can't even believe I'm thinking what I'm thinking. I mean, I've known Vickie and Edward since forever and it's really crazy and I shouldn't let my imagination get carried away like this. But I can't help it. I mean, I just started thinking and I think—"

"What?"

She hesitated. I stepped even closer. "Look, I know it's a little crazy to think of me as a private detective.

Sometimes even I have a hard time thinking of myself as a private detective. I don't look like a private detective. I don't always act like a private detective. In fact, I'm not a full-time private detective. But I've investigated enough cases to know there are things people see and things people think . . . and sometimes, when you consider what you saw and what you think, you're pretty sure you're imagining things, that you're just nuts. But then sometimes, when you talk it out with somebody, you realize it's not so nuts after all. What you're thinking, Beth, it might be way off base. But it might lead us to something that makes more sense. Or it might be right. I know that's sometimes hard to accept. But if you are right, don't you owe it to Vickie to try and find the truth? No matter what?"

Beth nodded. Her nose was red. She rubbed it and blubbered, "When you asked about Edward . . . I don't know, it just made me think, that's all. You see, when I left the sauna and came back inside, Edward's wineglass was on the table, but he was nowhere in sight. I asked Michael where he was and he said that Edward had stepped outside to smoke a cigar." She made a face. "Vickie hated those cigars, but he's never even tried to quit. I thought . . ." She shrugged. "Well, of course I didn't think anything of it. Until Celia brought you into the house."

It didn't take a detective to see where this was going. "You think . . . Edward?"

"He's a good friend of Celia and Scott's. He's been around here enough to know that the sauna's been acting funny and maybe that means he knows how to make it do whatever it did to get so hot so fast. If he knew you were inside and if he knew where the lock was . . . well, really, that wouldn't be all that hard because the lock was right there on that big rock outside the door of the sauna and anybody could have seen it." Her voice was as watery as her eyes. "I don't know how, but he know why you've been hanging around, Annie. He must know you've been asking questions. You know, about Vickie's murder."

I followed my own advice and talked out as much as I could of what I thought Beth was thinking, just to see where it would take me. "You think Edward knows I'm a PI. And that he knows I want to find out who killed Vickie. And that he tried to kill me because he thinks I'm getting close to the truth because . . ." No dice. As much as I tried, I knew I couldn't get past the very real objections to mesh with Beth's theory. "There's no way. He has an alibi. I checked it out. He was at that coaches' meeting the night Vickie was killed, and according to the minutes of the meeting, he didn't leave. He was there at the beginning, and he was there at the end." I thought about everything Tyler had said about murder. And marriage. "The police think it's somehow possible that Edward might have murdered Vickie, but . . . But you think . . . you think he killed her, too?"

"I don't just think it," Beth said, and she nodded like a bobble-head. "I know it for certain. And"—she burst into tears—"it's all my fault!"

IT TOOK A WHILE TO GET BETH CALMED DOWN. I found a plastic cup, poured some water, and made her drink, then I led her into the playroom and plunked her down on one of those video chairs. I sat in the one next to her, already worried about how I was going to get out of it again. When it stopped wobbling enough for me to think straight, I got down to business.

I pinned her with a look and wondered if she could even see me through her teary eyes.

"You seem pretty certain about Edward being guilty," I said. "You want to tell me why? And why do you think it's your fault?"

Beth started crying all over again. "Because . . ." The word bubbled past her tears. "Because I'm the one who told him about Vickie and Alex."

"Whoa!" I held up one hand to stop her in her tracks. There was only so much I could process at any one time, and this was a biggie. I leaned forward. My chair swayed. "You knew about Vickie and Alex? But I thought one of the rules was—"

"That we never discussed what we did on Tuesday nights, not even with each other. That's right." Beth wiped a finger under nose. "We always followed the rule, too. Every one of us. But then a few weeks ago, Vickie and I were working on the girls' Girl Scout cookie project. You know, tallying up sales and filling out order forms and deciding where we were going to put all those cases of cookies when they were delivered. I admit it, I was pretty overwhelmed by the whole thing. That kind of stuff always knocks me for a loop."

"And Vickie?"

"Vickie was never fond of numbers. She used to say . . ." Beth smiled through her tears. "Vickie used to say that the only good number is a dead number. Silly, but that gives you some idea about how she felt about math. But that day, even though we were counting and adding and balancing orders against how much money people owed, Vickie was in such a good mood, I couldn't believe it. She was humming and smiling. I asked her what was up. And she said . . ."

"Alex." Beth didn't need to confirm or deny. Apparently the way Vickie felt about Alex meshed with the way he felt about her. And the timing sounded right, too. According to Alex, he'd been meeting Vickie at Swallows for a few weeks.

Beth plucked at the skirt of her jumper. "It wasn't supposed to happen," she whispered. "Nobody ever meant it to. Going out on Tuesdays and meeting guys, it was just supposed to be a way for us to be ourselves. You know, without even our friends looking over our shoulders or judging our behavior. Nobody was ever supposed to fall in love."

It wasn't what she said, it was the way she said it. And the way she looked when she was talking, too. Suddenly there was a whole new sadness in Beth's eyes. When she leaned back into the video chair, she looked tired and disappointed.

Call me Dr. Phil, I knew exactly where this was going. "Vickie wasn't the only one, was she? You fell in love with someone you met on a Tuesday night, too."

One corner of Beth's mouth thinned. "I never told anyone. Not anyone but Vickie. I mean, it was perfect, wasn't it? She had a secret and so did I. And we were both dying to share our news. Oh." She blanched. "I didn't mean that. Not about the dying."

"It's OK. I know what you mean. You were excited. What did Vickie tell you about Alex?"

She shrugged. "Not much. She said he was handsome and funny, and that he had the most incredible accent. He's Scottish, you know."

I did. I nodded.

"Vickie said she knew we weren't supposed to go back to the same bar two weeks in a row, but that she just couldn't help it. She couldn't wait to see Alex again. I told her . . ." She looked away and lowered her voice, embarrassed. "I told her that's exactly how I felt about Jack. You know, the guy I met."

"Was Vickie going to divorce Edward? Do you think that's why he killed her?"

"I don't think Vickie and Alex's relationship had gotten that far. I mean, I know it hadn't between me and Jack. It was just fun, you know? Exciting. I loved the thought that he would be waiting for me every Tuesday at Preston's Colonial House. Don't get the wrong idea!" she added quickly. "It's not that I don't love Michael to pieces. I do. I love him. And the kids. I adore my kids. I love the life we have together. But being with Jack . . ." A shiver snaked over her shoulders. "Being with Jack makes me feel alive and excited. That's what Vickie said about spending time with Alex, too. That's why . . ." Beth stared straight ahead at the blank TV screen. Color raced into her cheeks. She looked at me out of the corner of her eye. "You're not going to tell anyone about this, are you?"

"I can't make that promise. At least not until you tell me more. But I can . . ." I reached out to touch a hand to her arm. My chair bucked, and maybe I had some residual weakness from the sauna incident; my head spun and so did the room. I waited until it settled down before I said, "If it doesn't have anything to do with solving the case, I swear I'll never breathe a word. If it does, I'll tell only the people who absolutely have to know. If you have a secret, Beth, it's safe with me."

I guess I'm pretty convincing. Or maybe I just have an honest face. Beth sighed and said, "Jack and I wanted to spend a night together. I know, I know . . . I know it's sleazy. And some people would say it's wrong. But I wasn't talking about running off with him and leaving my family and never taking care of them again. It was just one night." Fresh tears welled in her eyes. "It was just supposed to be one, fun night."

None of this meshed with the way I thought about Beth. But then, if I'd learned nothing else in the detective business, it should have been not to judge a book—or a person—by its cover. Embroidered teddy bears sometimes masked the beating of a passionate heart. "What happened?" I asked.

"I couldn't pull it off on my own. You know what I mean." I didn't, but I didn't let on. "I told Vickie what Jack and I were planning. I asked her to help me out. I told her that I was going to tell Michael that after cooking class that Tuesday, I was going over to Vickie's to help with the Girl Scout cookie order. That way, I could sneak back into the house early the next morning, climb into bed, and Michael would never know the difference. I'd just tell him that I'd gotten home from Vickie's really late."

"Did it work?"

Beth's expression soured. "Yes. And no. My Jeremy called Vickie's that Tuesday night I was with Jack. And Vickie told him I wasn't there."

"But why? You were friends. Why would Vickie—"

"Honestly, I don't know. I mean, I loved Vickie to pieces, but she could be bitchy with the best of them. I think she was jealous. She knew what Jack and I had planned that night—the suite at the Ritz, the champagne, the candlelit dinner—and she didn't have the nerve to do anything like that with Alex. She didn't have the guts to have any sort of real relationship with him. And she saw that I was willing to take a chance. She wanted Michael to find out what I was up to."

"And did he?"

"Michael?" Beth's laugh was watery. "Michael's easy

to fool. I didn't know any of this was going on, of course, so the next morning when I got up and Michael asked me where I was when Jeremy called, I'll tell you, it really knocked me for a loop. I was so nervous, I dropped the box of cereal I was holding and spilled Cheerios all over the floor. Good thing, too. By the time I was done cleaning them up, I had come up with a story for Michael. I just told him that Vickie was all mixed up, that by the time Jeremy called, I'd already left Vickie's and that I stopped to see another friend on the way home." She waved a hand. "He bought it hook, line, and sinker. Besides, Michael's been so preoccupied with the whole thing about getting a promotion, I don't think he would have noticed if I walked into the kitchen that morning wearing the same see-through red negligee I wore for Jack the night before."

That was more information than I needed. At the same time I tried to erase the picture from my head, I glommed onto part of what she said. Thinking about that piece of the puzzle was better than wondering if see-through red negligees came with embroidered teddy bears.

I narrowed my eyes and gave Beth a careful look. "Are you telling me—"

"I mean I was pissed, that's what I mean." Beth shot out of her chair, paced to the far side of the room, and came back again. "I was so mad at Vickie for what she tried to do to me that I called Edward and I . . ." She bucked up her courage. "I told him everything. Everything I knew about Alex and Vickie."

"Wow." It was anticlimactic at best, but I couldn't help myself. I pulled myself out of my chair, too. Or at least I tried. It took a couple pushes and a whole lot of thigh muscle twinging before I was on my feet. "That's why you think Edward killed Vickie. He knew she was seeing Alex."

"Uh-huh." Beth clutched her hands together at her waist. "And I just figured they'd have some big fight and that would be the end of it. But then Vickie ended up dead."

"And Michael ended up with a promotion."

Beth looked miserable before. Now she looked positively wretched. The waterworks started again. "Yes, yes, I admit it. I'm a low-down dirty scumbag. See, what I did is I mentioned something to Edward at the funeral, something about how much Michael deserved that promotion and how it would be smart if Edward gave it to him. And I tried to be really cool when I said it, you know? I didn't come right out and say *or else*. I was calm and collected. But I guess my hints weren't good enough. Edward acted like he didn't know what I was talking about. So I wrote him a note. And I couldn't make it look suspicious, so I put it inside a sympathy card to him and mailed it to the house. I told him he had to give Michael that job, that if he didn't, I'd go to the cops and tell them that he knew Vickie was spending her Tuesdays with Alex. It sounds terrible, I know, but Michael's worked so hard and that whole thing about that big scandal that he was responsible for . . . none of that was true. He's a good man."

"And you were feeling guilty for stepping out on him."

She nodded. "I figured getting that promotion for him was the least I could do for Michael. And . . ." She twisted the skirt of her jumper in nervous fingers. "I made Edward let Jeremy play in the soccer games, too."

So I was right about the blackmail. It made sense

from every angle. I shifted my gaze back to Beth. "And now?" I asked.

"Now you'd better be careful," she wailed. "Because if Edward knows that you know he killed Vickie, he's going to try to kill you again."

Twelve

■■

AFTER AN EVENING AS EXCITING AS THE ONE I'D just had, believe me when I say all I wanted to do was go home, jump into bed, and pull the covers over my head. Unfortunately, as often happens when I'm in the middle of an investigation, reality tends to intrude. What with visiting Sonny and following Celia, Glynis, and Beth, and nearly getting roasted to death, I hadn't put in nearly enough hours at Bellywasher's that week, and as much as I didn't want to think about it, I knew what that meant: Invoices were piling up on my desk like snowdrifts in Alaska. Bank deposits hadn't been made, and that meant we were losing out on interest. As little as it was, we needed every penny. If I didn't do something and do it fast, the well-oiled machinery of the business side of the restaurant was going to grind to a halt, and soon.

I might not feel like tackling the Bellywasher's checkbook, but never let it be said that Annie Capshaw is not nose-to-the-grindstone.

I left Celia's and by the time I got back to Old Town Alexandria, it was already late. Back in colonial times and even in the Civil War era, Old Town was a bustling Potomac port, just on the other side of the river from Washington, D.C. These days, its quaint cobblestone streets are lined with shops and restaurants and the entire town is a haven for tourists and weekend partiers. The area is an ideal spot for a pub like Jim's. But there's a downside to its popularity, too. Even on the best of days, parking is difficult. On Friday nights, it's a nightmare. In living color. And 3-D. I tried to be patient as I circled the block three times, but let's face it, being locked in a sauna and then having someone tell you that another someone wants to kill you . . . well, that tends to take the starch out of even the most plucky of detectives. By the time my virtue was rewarded and I found a parking space and dragged myself around the block and down the street to Bellywasher's, I didn't even care that I had to step aside and wait for a large party to leave the restaurant. Large parties mean big business. That lifted my spirits, sure enough. Besides, standing and waiting gave me a chance to rest, at least for a bit.

No sooner was I inside the restaurant, though, than every trace of fatigue disappeared. Jim was standing behind the bar. Eve and Tyler were there, too, and so was—

"Alex!" I couldn't cross the room and get over to the bar fast enough. Even as I practically tripped over my own feet, I caught Alex in an enormous bear hug. Just to be sure he was real and not some figment of my steamed-in-the-sauna imagination, I pulled myself out of his arms and gave him a careful look, then I hugged him again. "This is wonderful!" I didn't need to tell Jim and Eve. They were watching and smiling up a storm. I slipped onto the bar stool next to Alex's. "OK, somebody tell me what's going on. You didn't escape from jail or anything, did you? Did somebody smuggle you a file inside a cake?"

I was going for funny, but of course Tyler didn't appreciate the joke. He's that kind of cop. He was at the end of the bar and Eve was standing next to him with her hand on his shoulder. When someone called her over to ask for clarification about one of the menu items, she got to work and Tyler explained what was going on.

"You'll be happy to know that Alex is out on bail," he said. "With any luck . . ." He measured what he was going to say against the temptation of saying too much. Then, in a very un-Tyler-like moment that pretty much proved that, like the rest of us, he was relieved to have Alex back where he belonged, Tyler threw caution to the wind. "With any luck, all the charges against him are going to be dropped."

My breath caught behind the ball of mixed disbelief and excitement in my throat. I pressed a hand to my heart. "That's fabulous!" With one hand, I patted Alex's shoulder. With my other hand, I reached across the bar, grabbed onto Jim's, and gave it a squeeze. "Explain. Somebody tell me what happened. Tyler, did you guys finally find the real killer?"

"No such luck." Tyler's words cast a pall over the celebration. He grimaced. Jim frowned. Alex was deep in thought. He had a frothy dark beer in front of him, and he sipped it and licked the foam from his lips.

"Nectar of the gods!" Alex crooned, and as quickly as the mood darkened, it brightened again, and we all laughed. Beer was such a simple pleasure, and it was such a joy to watch Alex savor it! "They finally know I didn't do it, Annie," he said. "The medical examiner says the murderer was right-handed."

I would have slapped my forehead if Jim hadn't put a glass of white wine in front of me and if I didn't already have it in my hand. I looked to Tyler for confirmation. "The wounds—"

"Definitely made by a right-handed person, and one who's a whole lot shorter than Alex. We couldn't know for sure, of course, until the medical examiner's final report was in. The killer—"

"After Alex passed out, the killer put the knife in Alex's hand to implicate him, but he put it in his right hand!" I was so happy Tyler didn't point out that I was wrong, tears sprang to my eyes. "The killer couldn't possibly have known Alex was a leftie. So we know Alex was framed."

Far be it from Tyler to let anybody get too carried away. Especially when that anybody was me. "We're pretty sure," he said, in a way that told me *pretty sure* didn't mean *definitely* and I'd better not forget it. "But Alex isn't out of the woods yet. We still have some details to work out. For instance . . ." He spun his bar stool so that he was looking at Alex head-on, and slipped into interrogator mode so quickly and effortlessly, it was uncanny. I knew he wasn't being hard-assed just to cause trouble. Tyler knew what kind of questioning Alex had been through, and what he was in for in the coming weeks. He was just trying to get Alex ready for what was to come.

"How about those threats you made?" Tyler asked. "That waitress . . ." Even though Tyler wasn't directly involved in the case, it was obvious he had an interest in the outcome. He pulled his leather-covered notebook out of his pocket, flipped through the pages, and read over his notes. "The waitress at Swallows is named Jennifer. She says she heard you say that you wanted Vickie dead."

It was clear Alex had spent the long, dull hours in jail trying to work through this problem. It was just as clear that no matter how hard he tried, he was no closer to finding a solution now than he had been then. He scraped a hand back and forth across his chin. "I never would'a threatened Vickie," he said. "You all know that. I liked Vickie. And I'd never speak like that to a woman. It's disrespectful. I never said I wanted Vickie dead. If I did, I would have been out of my head."

This time, I didn't let the wineglass stop me. I set it down and slapped my hand against the bar. "That's it, of course!" Even before I explained, Tyler had already caught on. I had a funny feeling that if Derek Harold had been within earshot, Tyler would have read him the riot act about being a lead detective on a case and missing something so obvious.

It took Jim and Alex a little longer to get it. But then, they're the ones with the accents that are nearly impenetrable, especially to us Americans. To Jim and Alex's ears, they didn't have an accent at all.

"Dead and head." I stared at Alex. "Say the words again."

"Dead. Head." That's what he said, only it came out sounding more like *daid* and *haid*.

Jim got it. I could tell by the sudden gleam in his eyes. Alex needed a little more help, and I gave it to him. "So Jennifer heard you say something about Vickie being out of her head—"

"Aye. That's right." Alex's eyebrows veed. "That's what I told her when she started acting daft. I said she was out of her head."

"And if Vickie hadn't been murdered, that would have been the end of that. Jennifer never even would have remembered the conversation. But Vickie was murdered, and because she waited on you two, people started questioning Jennifer. And by then, of course, she wasn't just thinking of a man and a woman at a table together in the restaurant. She knew you'd been arrested. Whether she was aware of it or not, she was thinking of Vickie as the victim and you as the murderer. So just naturally—"

"She thought she heard *dead* instead of *head*. To her ears, the words sounded alike. You Americans need more practice in the proper way of speaking." Jim grinned. "It makes great sense in a mixed-up sort of way."

"Happens all the time with witnesses." Tyler had a beer in front of him, too, and he took a drink.

Alex did, too. "Well, I've certainly learned my lesson," he said. "From this moment forward until the day I get back on the plane to go home again, I'm not leaving your house, Jim. I'm going to work on that—"

In all the excitement of the investigation, I'd forgotten about the renovations on the house. Too bad I remembered now and was so eager to hear more, I leaned too far forward and almost fell off my bar stool. Otherwise, Alex might have spilled the beans.

"Oh, no!" Laughing, Jim reached across the bar, grabbed my shoulders, and pulled me back in place.

"But I could drive Alex home tonight. And if he needed anything, I could take it over to him. That way he wouldn't have to leave the house." It was worth a try.

Jim wasn't buying it. "I've given my word that I will keep an eye on Alex. And you . . ." He had a beer, too, and he raised it in a gesture that was more a friendly warning than a toast. "You will mind your own business. Which might include murder, but definitely does not include snooping around the house."

I may have grumbled. Like anyone could blame me? It was hard to stay in a good mood when even Tyler

bought into the whole Annie-can't-see-the-house-before-
the-wedding scenario.

"I'd take you on a grand tour of that house of Jim's,"
Tyler grumbled, "if it would help us solve our case."

It was all the reminder we needed that there was a lot
to do and a long way to go before Alex could put the
experience behind him.

I drummed my fingers against the bar. "Beth thinks
Edward did it," I told Tyler. "But Edward has an alibi."

"Detective Harold thinks Alex did it," Tyler added.
"But forensic evidence seems to eliminate him."

I thought and drummed, drummed and thought. I
hadn't had a chance to update Tyler on the latest news so
I took the opportunity to catch him up. Since we'd talked
on the phone the day after Eve, Norman, and I followed
the women, he knew they were all stepping out on their
husbands, but what Tyler didn't know was everything I'd
just found out at the wine tasting that evening.

"Beth was angry at Vickie," I explained, leaning
across the bar so that I could keep the information private. "A couple weeks ago, Beth spent the night with
some guy she met at Preston's Colonial House, and Vickie
was supposed to cover for her. Vickie didn't." I listened
to my own words and my stomach soured. "To get even,
Beth told Edward Monroe about Vickie and Alex."

"And you just said it yourself," Tyler reminded me.
"Edward Monroe has an alibi. You just said something
else, too, Annie. You just said Beth was mad at Vickie."

"Sure she was. But that can't possibly mean anything."
Could it?

The idea bounced around my brain and when it was
done in there, it hit my toes and settled in my stomach,
souring it. I gulped. "You don't suppose—"

But I knew Tyler did, because he sat up like a shot.

"Do we know where Beth was the night Vickie was killed?"

"Probably back at Preston's with Jack." Even though Tyler hadn't come out and said it, I sat back, distancing myself from what he was thinking. "Beth isn't the type."

In spite of my protests, Tyler was all over the theory. "She's shorter than Alex, right?"

I couldn't deny this.

"Is she right-handed?"

I had to think hard, but I remembered watching Beth at the wine tastings, and I had to admit she was.

"It's worth pursuing, Annie," Tyler told me. He slipped off the bar stool. "You may not like it—"

"I don't." I shrugged. "It's hard to explain. But she's a mom. Just like Vickie was. And she was a friend of Vickie's. Sure, she was mad at Vickie for nearly blowing her cover the night she spent with Jack, but as it turned out, her husband never found out she was fooling around, anyway. So she might have been annoyed at Vickie, but—"

"How do you know her husband never found out?" Tyler pinned me with a look.

And all I could do was shrug again. "Beth said—"

"And you believe her?"

I wanted to. Don't ask me why. When it comes to investigations, I'm usually all about following the clues no matter where they lead. And I was as eager as anyone to get Alex completely off the hook and clear his name. More eager than most, since I had Jim to think about and I knew Jim wouldn't rest until even the slightest hint of scandal was removed from Alex's name. Sure, we knew now that Alex had been set up, but until the real killer was found, there would always be that doubt, always that whiff of memory that would remind people that Alex had once been involved with a murder investigation. Had he been exonerated? Had he gotten off on a technicality? Most people wouldn't remember. They'd only remember that he was involved.

Unless we found the killer.

But . . . Beth?

I slumped back on the bar stool, uneasy with what I had to say and knowing I had to say it anyway. "She's blackmailing Edward. She says Edward's guilty and she knows it. But—" A new thought occurred to me and, encouraged, I sat up again. "If she was guilty, the blackmail wouldn't work, would it? She couldn't blackmail Edward for being the murderer when she was the murderer. But it is working. She convinced Edward to give her husband a promotion. And Edward wouldn't have done that if he wasn't the guilty party. If Beth was guilty—"

"Maybe Edward's thanking her for doing him a favor."

As quickly as I was encouraged, I was disheartened again. "But she wears jumpers with teddy bears embroidered on them," I wailed. It wasn't much of a defense, not the kind Tyler could possibly understand, anyway, but he was kind enough not to point it out. He already had his cell phone in his hands and I watched him punch in a number, then say hello to Derek Harold and ask if they could get together and talk about something that might be important to the case.

Beth, a killer?

No matter how many different ways I looked at the theory, it just didn't fit. Not in my book, anyway. Nobody who felt as guilty about misplacing Girl Scout cookie money as Beth did could possibly be heartless enough to kill a friend.

Could she?

And could she also have tried to cover her tracks by trying to snow another friend, one who was looking to get to the truth?

It was not a pretty thought, but then, I didn't like to think that I could be fooled that easily.

Especially since it looked like it had worked.

AS IT TURNED OUT, I NEVER DID WORK ON THE Bellywasher's accounts that night. By the time Tyler left to go talk to Derek Harold, my brain was spinning. I promised myself that come hell or high water, I would go into the restaurant the next day and not leave again until my desk was cleared, and after offering Alex a ride home one more time (and having Jim put the kibosh on the offer one more time), I headed home.

It was late, but I couldn't sleep.

I couldn't even relax.

I suppose it might have been the fault of all the Reuben dip, but I liked to think it was because my brain just wouldn't settle down. What with thinking that Alex was finally out of jail, and Beth was blackmailing Edward, and Beth might be the killer . . .

Is it any wonder I paced my apartment, too fidgety to keep still?

Finally, near midnight, I'd decided I'd had enough. If I was going to stay up all night, I might as well put the time to good use.

As far as I could see, at that time of the night, and closing in on the date of my wedding, the best use I could find for the long hours of the night was coming to a decision about that Scottish dish I wanted to make as a surprise for Jim.

I'd just gone to my computer to do a search, when I remembered Beth's magazine. It was on the counter in the kitchen, exactly where I'd left it the day I brought it home, and I hurried in there, fully prepared to find the answers to the culinary mysteries that had been dogging me.

I would have, too.

If when I picked up the magazine and paged through it, something didn't flutter out and hit the floor.

Even before I bent down to retrieve it, I knew what it was. But then, the envelope had landed faceup and I'd bought enough Girl Scout cookies in my day to recognize the familiar logo.

It looked like Edward Monroe was right, after all. How depressing was that?

Not only had I absconded with Beth's magazine, I'd stolen her Girl Scout cookie money, too.

Thirteen

✖

"A PHOTO ALBUM WOULD BE A PERFECT FAVOR!"
Apparently, Eve thought so, because even as she stepped around me and into my apartment, she whisked just such an album out of her leather tote bag and handed it to me. Since I already had my purse in one hand (not incidentally, Beth's Girl Scout cookie money was inside it) and my keys in my other hand, I back stepped toward my coffee table so I could set them down.

"We could talk about it later," I suggested to Eve. "I've got some things I have to do."

"Things that are more important than your wedding?"

I managed a smile. No easy thing since guilt had been eating at me all night and I hadn't gotten a wink of sleep. "Of course nothing's more important than my wedding," I told her, and I meant it. Only I didn't bother to mention that cleansing my conscience was plenty important, too, and that I'd never be able to do that until I explained the mix-up to Beth and threw myself on her mercy. "It's just that this has to do with the investigation and—"

"Then it can wait. Especially now that Alex is out of jail." She flopped down on my couch and I cursed myself for giving in and opening the door to her when I could have stepped out into the hallway, told her I was on my way out, and been done with it. "This is such a fabulous idea, I think we need to jump on it really soon."

"A photo album." I turned it over in my hands. The album was big enough to hold four-by-six prints. It had a shiny, satin-looking cover in a shade of ivory that appealed to me and, according to the sticker on the cover, each album could be custom embroidered with the names of the happy couple and the date of their wedding. "It's a good idea, but the wedding is one week from today."

"No buts. Look at how perfect this is." Eve plucked the album out of my hands. When she paged through it, I wasn't surprised to see it was filled with pictures of Doc. Doc on Eve's couch. Doc seated on one of the chairs at Eve's dining room table. Doc in her kitchen. Doc looking over the bottles of bubble bath in the bathroom closet, as if he was all set to choose a scent. In every picture, he was wearing a little red sweater that matched the one Eve had on.

I checked out each picture again. I looked over at Eve just in time to see her grin. "You're starting to get the picture. Picture! Get it?" With one elbow, she poked me in the ribs. "I took these pictures of Doc this morning. Every single one of them. But I still managed to get them all into a photo album, and you're wondering how, right? I took my camera over to that photo place on Wilson and *voila*! They had the whole album ready in just a couple minutes. Wouldn't that just be the best! We could take pictures during the ceremony—"

"You can't take pictures during the ceremony. You're the maid of honor."

"Well, not me, then. Norman."

"Norman is going to be the usher. He's going to show people where to sit and keep things in order."

"Well, somebody else then." Eve dealt with the objection with a toss of her head. "Anyway, there could be pictures taken. By *somebody*. And as soon as the ceremony is over and the reception starts, that same *somebody* could run out with the camera and come back with the albums. It's a great idea."

In the scheme of Eve's wedding planning ideas, it wasn't bad. It was unobtrusive, didn't involve sparklers, and there had been no mention of Doc actually taking part in the ceremony, resplendent—or not—in a tux. I was almost convinced until I saw the price list stuck into the back of the photo album. I multiplied the cost of the albums times the number of people who said they'd be honored to join us. Even though we'd vowed to keep the wedding small and the guest list to a limit, the total was staggering.

"Simple, Eve. Remember?" Since I couldn't believe my eyes, I'd pulled the price list out of the album for a better look. Now I handed it back to her. "I know math isn't your thing, so take my word for it when I tell you we'd need our own bailout to make this work. I refuse to go into debt for this wedding. We've got house renovations to think about. And there's no way I'm going to use any of the money earmarked for Bellywasher's expenses. I won't do that. Not to Jim. That pub means the world to him."

"You're right." Eve gave in with her usual good grace. She puckered her lips, thinking. "We could sell them at the door. You know, not for a profit. Just for cost."

I didn't honor this suggestion with a reply. Instead,

I grabbed my purse and keys, got up, and headed for the door. I would have liked nothing better than to have Eve's company on the drive to McLean, but truth be told, I was still too mortified by my unwitting theft of Beth's money to admit it to anyone. Once I gave the money back . . . once Beth and I laughed about the crazy situation . . . once she forgave me . . . then I might feel better about telling the story to Eve and to everybody else. For now, I'd have to settle for driving to McLean by myself.

The better to practice my apologies all the way there.

Fortunately, Eve had to get to Bellywasher's to handle the Saturday lunchtime crowd, so giving her the slip was no problem. A half hour later, I'd parked my car (my real car, the Saturn, since I didn't have to pretend to be a neighbor anymore and Norman was using his Jag for a personal appearance that day, anyway), and headed up the driveway toward the house.

"You're not going to believe this!" One last time, I went over what I wanted to say, even though I'd already gone over it a dozen times before. I stopped to try it on the bear and the moose on that *Welcome Friends* sign near the front door. "The craziest thing happened when I was here for the wine tasting a week ago."

Yeah, it sounded good. But that didn't keep me from cringing. After all, if I admitted that the envelope with the cookie money inside was tucked into the cooking magazine, I'd also have to admit that I'd pilfered the cooking magazine. It wasn't the end of the world, but it was enough to make a person as honest as me shake in my shoes.

I was trembling when I rang the bell, and I'd been so

worked up about the whole thing, I'd never even considered what I would do if Beth wasn't home.

But she wasn't.

Nobody was.

Nobody answered.

More disappointed than relieved, I turned away from
the door. As painful as it would have been, I wanted to get
the whole thing over with, and knowing I'd have to wait
for another opportunity and spend another who-knew-
how-many hours obsessing about the whole thing . . .
well, it wasn't a pleasant prospect.

I decided to try one more time.

I turned back and rang the bell again.

There was still no answer.

I doubted Beth was hiding behind a potted palm,
watching the door and waiting for me to leave. For one
thing, I didn't remember seeing any potted palms in her
house. For another, she couldn't possibly have known
that Tyler and I had discussed the feasibility (or not) of
her being a suspect in Vickie's murder. There was no
reason for Beth to hide and not answer the door.

With that in mind, I pressed my nose to the long,
skinny pane of glass to the left of the front door.

And that's when I found out how very wrong I could be.

See, there was a very good reason for Beth not to answer the bell, and it had nothing to do with hiding because she might be a suspect.

When I looked inside, I saw all the beautiful art glass
on display at the bottom of the winding staircase had
been smashed to smithereens.

And Beth's body, broken and bleeding, in the middle
of it all.

* * *

TYLER IS NOT THE WARM AND FUZZY TYPE. WHICH means he wasn't gentle about it when he braced a hand at the back of my neck and forced my head between my knees.

"Breathe," he said. "It's the only thing that's going to get rid of the light-headed feeling."

I wasn't so sure I believed him, but it's not like I had a lot of choice so I gave it a try. Except for the fact that my neck was killing me, after a minute or so, I did feel a little better.

At least a little better than I had since I scrambled for my phone and made a frantic call to McLean emergency services.

The paramedics had arrived in short order. So had the cops. Through it all and a haze of tears, I'd stood aside and kept out of the way, just like they told me to. I hadn't even realized I was swaying on my feet and nauseous, too, until Tyler showed up out of nowhere, told me to sit down, and proceeded to make sure I didn't throw up and spoil the pristine landscaping.

After a couple more minutes, the pressure of Tyler's hand decreased and I dared to raise my head. I was just in time to see the paramedics wheel Beth out on a stretcher. There was a white sheet over her face.

My stomach swooped again and this time, I didn't need Tyler to tell me what to do. I hung my head between my knees and tried to block out the clinking and clanking as the stretcher was loaded into the ambulance.

It wasn't until the ambulance pulled out of the driveway that I picked up my head. "What are you doing here?" It was a stupid question at a time like that, but I wasn't about to argue with my more sensible self. If I focused on facts, I could avoid thinking about everything I'd seen there in Beth's foyer, how that beautiful ecru tile had been dotted with color. Some of it was bits and pieces of Michael's art glass collection. More of it was blood. "How did you—"

"I just so happened to be having lunch with one of the guys I know on the McLean department, and I heard the call come in. I recognized Beth's name, and the address. I told my buddy whatever happened here might have something to do with a case I was working on."

"In other words, you lied." In other circumstances, I might have given him a one-upmanship smile. This time, I didn't even try. "Do you think it has something to do with Vickie's death? It can't be . . ." The word stuck in my throat. I cleared it away. "It can't be murder, can it?"

Tyler glanced toward the house. "Too early to tell," he said. "But I did hear a couple of the crime scene techs talking. There's evidence of what might have been a struggle at the top of the steps."

"Someone pushed her?" I closed my eyes, but that did nothing to erase the image that formed in my mind. I gulped down the sour taste in my mouth. "You think the two murders are related?"

"A little too coincidental if they're not."

"You thought Beth murdered Vickie."

He sucked on his teeth, stalling before he admitted he was wrong. "It was a theory. I never said I knew it for certain."

"But Beth couldn't have been the murderer. Not if someone murdered her."

"We're getting way ahead of ourselves." Tyler sat down on the porch steps next to me. The steps were wide and we were way off to the side, the better to keep to ourselves and not get in anyone's way. "Last night, you said Beth was blackmailing Edward Monroe."

I nodded. "She wanted her husband to get a promotion. And she wanted her son to play soccer, too. Edward's the team coach, and Jeremy's an awful soccer player. She said that if Edward didn't let Jeremy play—"

Tyler held up a hand to stop me. "Are you saying she was blackmailing him about soccer? It's that important?"

"To these people it is. It all is. Where they live and who they know and what their kids have accomplished. Or not accomplished. Do you think Edward could have killed Beth?"

"Can't say. It's way too early to tell." He looked like he wished he could say more. "But I'll let my friend on the force here know what's been going on. I'll tell him to check out Monroe's alibi. And the whole blackmailing angle. I don't suppose you have any proof that Beth was telling the truth about that?"

"Not a shred. She did say she mentioned it to Edward and he acted like he didn't know what she was talking about. So she wrote him a note. She tucked it in a sympathy card she sent after Vickie's death." The look I gave him was hopeful. "I don't suppose—"

"That he kept it? Nobody's that stupid." Tyler looked disappointed that it was true. He stood. "That doesn't mean the local guys can't check it out. In fact—"

He stopped midsentence when a car sped into the driveway. Its driver, Michael, slammed on the brakes, then got out and raced over to the nearest police officer.

"Someone called me at my club," Michael stammered. "They said something was wrong. What happened? It's not . . . one of the kids? Beth?"

A detective who was standing nearby took Michael by the arm and walked him over nearer to where we waited. They spoke quietly, but I knew what they were saying. I watched, my heart breaking, as the news registered. Michael's face went ashen. His eyes glazed over. "No!" The word dissolved into an anguished cry. "It can't be true," he sobbed. And then he said something else, something I didn't quite catch, but something that sounded a whole lot like—

I told myself not to get carried away. I remembered the whole mix-up about Alex and *dead* and *head*. I warned myself that same sort of thing might very well be what was happening here: I was hearing one thing and thinking it was something else. That had to be it. It was the only thing that made any sense. Still . . .

I know for certain that I saw Michael stare at the open front door of his house and all that smashed glass that lay just beyond. And I was just as sure I heard him mumble something, something that sounded a whole lot like "This wasn't supposed to happen yet."

REAL OR NOT, THE COMMENT SENT MY IMAGINA-tion into overdrive. I didn't dare bug Michael about it that day. I mean, he'd just found out that his wife was dead. There didn't seem to be much use in trying to talk to him, and it would have been cruel besides. I bided my time, and I did manage to catch up on my work at Bellywasher's, but only because I went in on Sunday and stayed until every last check was paid and every last account was balanced.

That left me free to attend the calling hours for Beth on Monday.

Of course Celia and Glynis were there and of course they looked shell-shocked, as might be expected. Losing one friend is hard enough. Having two die and in such short succession . . . well, I'd barely known Beth, and I hadn't known Vickie at all, and even I was bursting into tears at the drop of a hat. We hugged, and talked, and I made my way toward the tasteful urn displayed on a table and surrounded by photos and mementos. Since I didn't want to cause a fuss, I made sure to stay clear of Edward. He was over in one corner, talking quietly to Scott. I scanned the room, looking for Chip, Glynis's husband, and found him sitting in another corner by himself. He was weeping.

I wasn't heartless enough to disturb his grief, so like the dozens of other people there before me, I waited in a long receiving line to pay my respects and extend my condolences to Michael. Unlike any of the others, I had an ulterior motive. After I told Michael how sorry I was and how much I was going to miss Beth (both true), I made my move.

"I don't know if you remember, Michael, and I can certainly understand if you don't. But I was the one who found Beth on Saturday. I stopped by, and I saw her through the front window. I'm the one who called 911."

"Yes, of course." Behind his Coke-bottle glasses, Michael blinked as if he was trying to replay the scene in his head and find where I fit in. "You were there. On the front porch when I arrived home. It never registered."

"You had other things to think about."

He nodded. "Maybe it's just that I wasn't all that surprised to see you. These days, you always seem to be around when bad things happen."

It was hard to deny, even if it was a little hard to take. I swallowed down a reply that was a little too terse for the occasion. "I happened to be listening when the police talked to you," I said, "and you said something curious.

I've been wondering about it ever since, and I've just got to ask. When they told you Beth was dead, you said, 'This wasn't supposed to happen yet.'"

"Did I? I honestly can't remember." There was that blink again. Michael reminded me of an agitated owl. He shook his head as if to clear it and looked past me to the next person in line, dismissing me as easily as that.

Not to worry, I wasn't about to be brushed off so quickly. I pretended to be oblivious and I kept my place. "It just seems so odd. I can only imagine what you must have been feeling. And I think at a time like that, I might say something like *oh, no* or *please, tell me it's not true.* Even *this wasn't supposed to happen* makes sense to me, because of course, it wasn't. Beth was loved by her friends and her family. She's going to be missed. What happened to her shouldn't happen to anyone. But it's that one little word. That *yet . . .*"

Michael blanched. I was pretty sure he was going to roll up in a ball and crumple to the floor until something behind me caught his eye. I turned to see that Edward Monroe was looking our way. When I turned again to Michael, he pulled back his shoulders and lifted his chin.

"Of course it wasn't supposed to happen yet," he snapped. "Beth and I were supposed to live a long life together. We were going to grow old together, retire together, watch our great-grandchildren grow up. You understand that, don't you, Annie? It wasn't supposed to happen *yet.*" He drew out the word so I had plenty of time to think about it. "No one's supposed to die that young."

"Of course." What else could I say? With another smile tinged with just enough sympathy to be sincere but not too cloying, I backed away.

And headed straight for the door.

Did I believe Michael? Sure, everything he told me made sense, but that didn't mean I was going to take it all at face value. This was my perfect opportunity not only to do a little digging, casewise, but to do what I'd gone to McLean on Saturday to do in the first place.

I left the funeral chapel and within a couple minutes, I was parked around the corner from Beth and Michael's house, the better to make sure my car wasn't spotted. I hurried up the driveway and peeked in the windows. There was no one around.

And remember, there was a hide-a-key.

The tantalizing thought flitted through my brain, teasing and tempting me. I glanced around the yard, trying to put myself in Beth's place, and in Celia and Glynis's, too, since they said they all kept keys hidden outside their homes. Under those fake rocks seemed a little too obvious. So did under the mat. (I know, because I looked and there was nothing there.) That left . . .

I stepped down from the porch and looked over the house, trying to think like a detective. If all the women had hidden keys, and each of them knew where the others' were, then it would make sense if they were all in the same sort of place. I had never been to either Vickie's or Glynis's house, but I'd driven by. Each house was as different and individual as each woman. Beth's was modern, Celia's was cottagey-cute. Vickie's was a sturdy Colonial much like the one I imagined for myself, and Glynis's was a sprawling monstrosity that looked more like a medical building than a house. In fact, there was only one thing each of the homes had in common.

My gaze lit on the *Welcome Friends* sign with the moose and the bear, and I knew my instincts were right on. As it turned out, there was a little door in the back of the sign, and inside that—

"The front door key!" I held it up triumphantly, but I knew I couldn't waste time. The calling hours at the funeral home wouldn't last forever. I raced inside the house. Ignoring the broken shelves that had once held Michael's glass collection and the smudges of dark color that still stained the floor tiles, I headed straight for the kitchen. The envelope with the Girl Scout cookie money in it was still in my purse and I pulled it out and looked for a place to put it. If I left it out on the kitchen countertop, it would be too obvious. I needed something more subtle, someplace Michael would think Beth had put the envelope and forgotten about it.

I found the perfect solution in the desk just outside the laundry room. Feeling as relieved as if I was dropping a weight from my shoulders, I slid open the top drawer, popped the envelope into place, and breathed a sigh of guilt-free relief.

That taken care of, I thought about what other kind of snooping I could do since I was already in the house, and wondered if perhaps Michael had a home office. The thought firmly in mind, I was just about to close the desk drawer when something under a pile of papers in it caught my eye. I reached for it, pulled it out, and found myself holding a small round coaster made of heavy card stock. The coaster featured a sepia-toned photograph of the sign that hung above the front door of the establishment it came from.

Swallows.

Fourteen

✖

THE NEXT DAY, EVE AND I WERE AT THE GROCERY store. She was being a good sport and hanging out with me on her lunch hour simply because I asked her to. And me? I was multitasking. The wedding was just four days away, my investigation was getting nowhere, and I hadn't had a spare moment to decide on a Scottish dish to serve at our wedding dinner. It all needed to be taken care of, so in my own perfectly logical way, I decided the best way to get it all done was to do it all at once.

I'd been so intrigued by the Swallows coaster I found in the kitchen desk at Beth's, I'd forgotten to return the cooking magazine that I had every intention of putting back along with the Girl Scout cookie money. The way I saw it, that was a sign. Eventually, I'd make copies of all the Scottish recipes in the magazine, then pop the whole thing (anonymously, of course) in the mail. Until then, I figured some higher power somewhere intended me to use the magazine. I'd grabbed it from my kitchen counter that morning on my way out my door.

I'd stuck a sticky note on the page where the article about Scottish foods began. Now, standing in the middle of the dairy aisle, I flipped open the magazine, closed my eyes, and stabbed a finger on the page. "I'm going to make whatever recipe I'm pointing to," I told Eve, and since it was something she would have done herself—say, to choose between two dresses she wanted in the newest issue of *Vogue*—she never questioned my decision process. I opened my eyes and read the heading above the recipe where my finger rested.

"Crappit heid." I cringed, closed my eyes, and tried again. This time, at least I didn't point to a recipe we'd already considered—and rejected. I read out loud, "Haggis, the most Scottish of dishes."

It sounded promising, at least from the headline. I can only attribute my lack of reading comprehension to that and the fact that I was in a hurry, and feeling stressed. Jim and I were supposed to have our final, wrap-everything-up meeting with the florist that evening, and I had the final fitting for my wedding dress in just forty-five minutes, so I gave the recipe the most cursory of scans and pushed the grocery cart toward the back of the store, stopping along the way to load the proper ingredients into my cart.

"Cinnamon, nutmeg, coriander, pepper. Oh, salt, too," I read and tossed, and because the next ingredient on the list was oatmeal and I knew I'd find it two aisles over, we zipped over in that direction.

"Beef or lamb. That's what we need next. It says we can choose which we want to put in, beef or lamb." We were on the move, and Eve was reading over my shoulder, so I didn't question her. We rolled toward the meat department and while we were on our way there, I decided it was time to start killing those two birds with that one proverbial stone.

"Here's the thing," I said, getting back to what I'd wanted to talk about in the car on the way over, only Eve had been driving, and traffic was heavy. I was so busy hanging on for dear life, we hadn't gotten any further than me finally owning up to accidentally purloining the Girl Scout cookie money and telling her what I found in the desk in Beth's kitchen the night before. We simply hadn't had enough time to draw any conclusions. "Why would Michael have a Swallows coaster?"

"He picked it up as a souvenir?" Leave it to Eve to be literal.

"Well, he did. He must have. Or Beth did." This was a new thought, and while I considered it, we arrived at the meat department and I consulted the recipe again, carefully this time. I read out loud. "One sheep's stomach, cleaned thoroughly, scalded, turned inside out, and soaked overnight in salted water. The heart and lungs from one lamb. Stock made from boiling the lungs." I didn't have to look at Eve. I knew she had turned as green as I was. In an uncharacteristic move, I left the grocery cart right where it was and, side by side, we raced out of the store.

WE DUBBED IT THE HAGGIS INCIDENT, AND VOWED never to speak of it again.

Keeping the thought firmly in mind, just a little while later I was standing in front of the full-length mirror at Marie's, the bridal shop where I'd bought my dress, and we were talking about everything but. It wasn't hard. I was pleased to death with my dress. It fit like a dream and thinking about what Jim would say when I walked into Bellywasher's on my dad's arm and Jim saw me in the dress for the first time, I grinned.

But of course, I had other things on my mind, too. Things other than boiling sheep lungs in saltwater and (gulp!) what's actually involved in turning a scalded stomach inside out.

Like that coaster from Swallows. That was something we needed to discuss.

"Here's the thing . . ." I turned this way and that, checking myself out in the mirror and deciding that I'd definitely made the right decision by choosing the peach-colored dress. It was plain enough to satisfy the pragmatic me, and the beaded collar of the bolero added just enough bling to make it a special occasion dress. "Doesn't it seem a little odd that he'd have it? One of his wife's best friends had just been killed there, and according to what Tyler found out, Michael never told the police anything about going to Swallows or even knowing where it was."

Eve was more interested in the hemline on my dress than she was in the investigation. She stepped back, eyeing it carefully to make sure it was even. "Maybe he forgot."

I wasn't buying it. "The coaster was hidden."

"It was under a pile of papers. That's what you said. That doesn't exactly mean it was hidden. Maybe it was just forgotten."

"Maybe." I frowned. "Maybe Beth wasn't the only one who knew that Vickie was meeting Alex over at Swallows. Maybe Michael knew it, too. But if he did, why would he care?"

I might have gotten an answer—of any sort—from Eve if she hadn't heard someone walk by outside the dressing room and chosen that moment to stick her head out the door. One of the clerks had a load of dresses in her arms; I saw a flash of rhinestones and a shimmer of color.

"Oh!" Caught by the sparkle and splendor, Eve stepped into the hallway. "I'd like to try that one, and that one, and that one," I heard her say. "In a six. Unless you think that might be a little snug on me."

I pictured the clerk looking Eve up and down before she said, "It might be just a tad too big," and because, of course, that was exactly what Eve wanted to hear, she was smiling when she stepped back into the dressing room.

"You look really pretty, honey," Eve said. "That color is perfect on you."

"I don't know." I checked the mirror again. "I love the color, but maybe white or ivory—"

"Good gravy, Annie! White or ivory is for first weddings. And old frumps. This is a celebration, honey. What you need is a really pretty party dress. And that—"

I spun in front of the mirror and smiled back at my reflection. "It's a really pretty party dress, isn't it? In fact, it's perfect!"

It was, and I was grateful that the dress was truly comfortable, and I wouldn't have trouble moving, or dancing, or raising one of those champagne glasses to toast while I was wearing it. "I had ivory for my first wedding. This is different. It's understated, but it's special, too. You think Jim will like it?"

Her raised eyebrows said it all.

Mine rose just as far when the clerk brought an armful of dresses in the room for Eve. She still hadn't decided on a dress to wear for the wedding, but seeing the

wash of bright colors, I cringed. I had been thinking
something nice and conservative and understated for my
maid-of-honor. What Eve was thinking was anybody's
guess.

The first dress was red velvet and just long enough to
maybe hit the knees of someone half Eve's height. There
were ostrich feathers around the hemline. I caught my
breath while Eve held it at arm's length to look it over,
and I let go a covert sigh of relief when she set the dress
down.

The second dress was a pretty color, deep sapphire
blue, but a little too dramatic for my taste. Then again, I
was pretty sure it was a little too dramatic for anything
except maybe a little theater production of *Gone with the
Wind*. The gown was strapless, and it had a bodice just
dripping with rhinestones and a wide skirt that was
ruched up all over so that it looked like frothy little
mounds of blue whipped cream. That one, too, Eve set
aside.

The third dress—

When Eve held it up to look it over, I hardly dared to
move or breathe. The dress was chiffon with a swingy
skirt and it had a halter-type top, but like mine, it was a
tasteful little number, knee-length and dressy without
being flamboyant. Yes, there were rhinestones, but not
too many, just a sprinkling of them at the waist and down
one side of the skirt. Not too overdone. Not too dazzling.
And not so sparkly that the dress would blind anyone
when Eve walked down the makeshift aisle we were
planning to set up from the front door of Bellywasher's
to the bar. The best part? The dress was peachy, just a
couple shades darker than mine.

"What do you think?" Eve asked.

I didn't dare wax too poetic. If I did, she'd go for the

sapphire blue in a heartbeat. "You should try it on. It seems a little—"

"Too plain?" Eve wrinkled her nose. She gave the dress another look, then held it up in front of herself. "Does it make my complexion look sallow?"

"Absolutely not!" It was the truth and besides, I was secretly rooting for the peachy dress. It was everything I'd ever dreamed a bridesmaid's dress should be. "I'll bet if you try it on, you'll like it. I mean, it's that kind of dress, isn't it? It might not look like much on the hanger, but once you've got it on, pow! You know, it might just be one of those dresses that looks spectacular on. Why don't you—"

"No." Eve shook her head. Her gaze traveled back to the blue whipped-creamy dress and my spirits plummeted. She looked at the peachy one again and my hopes rose like those perky mounds of whipped cream. "I'm not going to try it on," she said, and before my hopes had a chance to take another dive, a smile cracked her solemn expression. "That's because I already did! I stopped in here two weeks ago and saw the dress. I tried it on then and fell in love with it just like that. It's already been altered and it's all ready to go. I swore Marie to secrecy about it. I knew you'd love it. I wanted to surprise you!"

Surprise me she did, and I found out for sure that I would be able to move freely while wearing my dress. Since I was standing on the platform in the center of the room, I didn't even have to reach up—at least not too much, anyway—to fold Eve into a hug. "You're the best friend in the world," I told her.

She brushed off the compliment. "It's easy to be a best friend in the world when you've got the best friend in the world to be best friends in the world with."

Semantics aside, we both knew we'd get all teary if we didn't change the subject. I carefully slipped out of my wedding dress and back into my jeans and black T-shirt. While Marie herself—beaming a big smile and proud of herself for the part she'd played in Eve's little deception—took both dresses to get them packaged and set to go, we sat in the dressing room and waited.

"So back to that coaster," I said, because honestly, I was beginning to feel as if we'd never get any further with the case if we didn't talk about it every chance we had. "Why wouldn't Michael mention that he'd been to Swallows? You'd think he'd tell the police."

"Unless he didn't want them to know."

"And he didn't want them to know because . . ." Here was the sticking point, and stick me, it did. Stuck, I propped my elbows on my knees and braced my head in my hands. "Maybe Edward wasn't the only one Beth blabbed to. Maybe she told her husband that Vickie was going over to Swallows every week to meet Alex."

"That doesn't seem likely, not when Beth was doing the same thing with that Jack guy. She had secrets, too, remember. I don't think she'd want to give her husband any ideas."

Eve was right. I acknowledged it with a tip of my head. "Maybe Michael killed Vickie." It was a bad idea; I knew that the moment the words left my lips. I tossed it out, anyway, for what it was worth and because I couldn't think of anything else to say.

"You mean, maybe Michael and Vickie were having an affair?" Eve cocked her head, considering the suggestion. "And he knew Vickie was seeing Alex, too? And he went over there, and in a jealous rage he killed Vickie?"

"And then he picked up a coaster as a souvenir." My shoulders slumped. I saw where she was going with her argument, but hey, I knew the theory was weak from the moment I mentioned it, so I wasn't too disappointed to watch it get shot down.

As usual, I didn't stay glum for long. "So let's look at it another way. If the coaster didn't belong to Michael, and it wasn't Beth's, maybe someone else left it there. That would be easy enough to do. Each of the friends knows where the others keep their hide-a-keys. And they're together at least once a week for the wine tastings, and their husbands come, too. Maybe someone left the coaster there as a kind of message to Michael or Beth."

Eve liked the sound of this. Her eyes sparkled. "That's brilliant, Annie! It's a message. I like that. What does the message mean?"

She had me there. Fortunately, I didn't have a chance to try to explain my brilliant theory. Marie showed up with both our dresses in garment bags and made me promise to show her lots of pictures from the wedding. Of course I agreed, and we left to get back over to Bellywasher's before the evening dinner crowd started to gather.

Did I mention that the dress shop is in Old Town Alexandria, not far from Bellywasher's? And that since it was a gorgeous spring day, the sidewalks were packed with tourists and locals out enjoying the sunshine? On our way back to the pub, we barely had a chance to walk next to each other, much less talk. When we stopped at a red light to cross a street, I waited for Eve to worm her way through the crowd to my side. Because I didn't want to lose her in the press, I'd just missed the last light, and

I toed the edge of the curb and tried not to get too annoyed when a lady behind me poked me with the corner of her very large purse.

When Eve finally found her way to me, I picked up right where I'd left off and knew she wouldn't miss a beat. That's what being best friends is all about. It was one of the reasons I knew she'd understand when I explained, "All these people . . . Vickie and Celia and Glynis and Beth . . . they were all best friends. And their husband are best friends, too. They've known each other forever, some of them work together, their kids all play together. That means Michael probably didn't kill Vickie. It just doesn't make sense. And I don't think Tyler's right about Beth killing Vickie, either. For one thing, that doesn't explain what happened to Beth."

Eve nodded. "So you think the same person killed them both."

"It makes sense." It did. It was one of the few aspects of the case that did. "So if we solve one murder, we'll solve the other. And I'd love to know why Edward fell for Beth's blackmail if he wasn't the one who killed Vickie, and if he is, I'd love to know how he did it in the first place when he was at that coaching meeting that night. And then there's Michael saying that Beth wasn't supposed to die yet. And Chip. He's miserable and yeah, a couple of his wife's friends have died, but that doesn't explain why he's so jumpy and—" Over to my left, across a side street from where we waited, a bus pulled away from the curb and, by force of habit, I took a step back.

That was the exact moment somebody put a hand to the small of my back and gave me a rough push. My feet went out from under me and though there wasn't anything for me to grab onto, my arms (and the garment bag with my wedding dress in it) flailed.

I tried, but it was impossible for me to keep my balance. With a yelp of surprise, I stumbled into the street.

And the only thing I saw when I did was that bus. It was coming straight at me.

IT ALL HAPPENED IN SLOW MOTION AND WITH THE combined cacophony of Eve's screams and the grinding gears of the bus as a sort of soundtrack to the scene.

The bus got nearer. I saw the driver's mouth drop open and his hands tighten around the wheel. I watched as a woman who'd just boarded the bus dropped her purse and put her hands over her eyes. That big ol' bus grille got closer and closer, so close I could see the spots of road dirt splattered over it, and one big bug who'd made a wrong turn midflight and ended up flatter than a pancake.

Just like I was about to do.

My brain froze the way people's do when they're suddenly in dire straits and they find themselves acting on instinct and instinct alone. It wasn't like I thought it would stop the bus or somehow ward off the thump I was about to feel when it hit me head-on, but I held up my hands.

The bus got closer.

I squeezed my eyes shut.

Then somebody grabbed my T-shirt and tugged me hard back onto the sidewalk.

I felt the hot breeze as the bus whizzed past, shook myself, and looked around. I was back up on the curb where I belonged, and Eve still had her hands bunched into the back of my T-shirt. The bus—

"Oh, no!" I screamed because it wasn't until the bus

had already gone by that I realized that in the excitement, I'd dropped the garment bag and it had gotten
caught under the wheels of the bus. Even as I watched,
horrified, the garment bag containing my wedding dress
got dragged down the street. My instincts took over
again, and I took off after the bus. I never got very far.
See above: Eve was hanging on for dear life, and there
was no way she was going to let me get away.

"It's too late, Annie," she said. "There's too much
traffic. And a dress isn't worth getting run over for."

This? From Eve, the woman who would have gladly
jumped in front of a bus—no matter how big—to save a
vital fashion accessory?

The fact that she was talking so much sense told me
exactly how upset she was.

Side by side, we stood and watched. At the next inter-
section, the garment bag pulled loose. Three cars ran
over it. The bag ripped open, and I saw a brief flutter of
fabric like a peachy surrender flag—right before a pickup
truck whizzed past. When the truck turned the corner in
front of us, there was a scrap of oil-stained, tire-marked,
tattered satin hanging from his bumper.

"My poor dress!" Tears sprang to my eyes, and I was
buffeted by the crowds of people who, now that the excitement was over, hurried to get by us and get across the
street. Had one of them pushed me? I looked around,
anxious to see if there was a familiar face in the crowd,
but by that time, it was already too late. If there was a
person in the crowd with murderous intent, he—or she—
was long gone.

"Oh, my dress!" At my side, Eve wailed and I put a
hand on her shoulder to comfort her.

"It's nice of you to take this so personally." I patted
her arm. "But really, Eve, it was my dress and—"

"No! Really!" She grabbed me and swung me all around so that I could look to our right, to our left, up and down the street. "Now it's *my* dress, too. I put my garment bag down to help you," she wailed.

And there was no sign of it. Not anywhere.

I honestly can't say what upset me more, my wedding dress getting run over, Eve's bridesmaid's dress getting stolen, or somebody trying to push me in front of a bus.

OK, maybe I can. I guess in the great scheme of things, getting smashed to smithereens pretty much takes the cake.

Fifteen

✖

IT WAS THE WHOLE BEST-FRIEND THING THAT GOT me thinking, and I had Eve to thank for that.

After all, who else but a best friend would have been game enough to venture out into Old Town Alexandria traffic with me, weaving, bobbing, and dodging to retrieve all that was left of my wedding dress? Who else would have tenderly carried those pieces of fabric to the nearest bus stop bench, then sat down next to me and cried right along with me?

Who else but Eve would have known that my disappointment was bound to morph into self-pity and chosen the exact right moment to vow (fist raised in the air like Scarlett O'Hara, but *sans* root vegetable) that, as God was her witness, she was going to do whatever it took to find me another dress in time for the wedding? And was there anyone else in the whole wide world who would move mountains to make sure it happened? Anyone but Eve? Absolutely not!

On top of all that, she'd had her own dress literally

swiped right out from under her because she'd gone above and beyond to save my life. Talk about a best friend!

She insisted, so I left all my wedding worries in Eve's capable hands and yes, I knew I was trusting a lot to a woman whose closet was filled with more froufrou then I'd ever owned or even knew existed. I had to. This was Eve, remember, and Eve had saved my life. She was my best friend.

Naturally, the whole best-friend thing got me thinking about Vickie and Celia and Glynis and Beth. And it got me thinking about their husbands, too. All the rest of that day and all that night, my brain spun with possibilities. I kept legal pads around for just such occasions and I filled their pages with scrawled notes, names, dates, times, and alibis. By the time the next day dawned, the brain power I'd expelled on the problem was rewarded—

I had a theory.

It was crazy, sure, but it was the only thing that fit. In fact, it was so improbable and outlandish, I didn't dare explain it to Jim, Eve, or Norman. Turns out, I didn't have to. I was cryptic. They were still game to help me out. After that, we worked together like a well-oiled machine. We decided the hours of Beth's funeral service were the safest to do a little undercover work, I told them where they'd find the women's hide-a-keys, and we put my plan into action.

Much to Norman's dismay, we didn't bring walkie-talkies. Instead, they each agreed to phone me during their searches. With any luck, it would be when they found what I hoped they'd find. I was already inside Vickie's house and carefully poking around Edward's study when the first call came in.

"Are you OK, Annie?" It was Jim, of course. Leave it

to the love of my life to worry about me more than about the case. He's a sweetheart.

"Of course I'm OK," I whispered. Don't ask me why. The family was at Beth's funeral and the house was empty and quiet. Besides, Edward's home office was straight out of every MBA candidate's dreams, from the mahogany desk and bookshelves to the carpet so plush, I sank into it when I crossed the room. Even if there was someone around, I could probably talk at the top of my lungs, and I wouldn't be heard. The place had that kind of Fortress of Solitude feel. Still, I wasn't one to take chances, and I kept my voice down. "I'm just about to look through Edward's desk."

"Well, I've already looked through this Michael fellow's desk." I'd sent Jim to Beth and Michael's. He wasn't happy about what he called trespassing, but I convinced him it was all in the name of clearing Alex's reputation, and bringing a killer to justice. "It seems you were right, Annie. I found—"

My phone beeped a call waiting. I told Jim I'd see him later. "Annie, you are the coolest PI since Mike Hammer!" It was Norman, who'd gone over to Celia and Scott's. I knew from the tone of his voice that he'd found what I was looking for, too. "How did you know?" he asked. "I mean, really, Annie, you are the bomb! I'm thinking we'll do an episode about you. You know, for the show. One night, it won't be the Cooking Con, it will be the Cooking PI. You could do a special guest appearance and you could show people how to make—"

Good thing Eve's call beeped in. It saved me from telling Norman *no way, no how*. Eve was at Glynis and Chip's, and as soon as she purred a cheery hello, I knew she'd had success, too. "I've got it, Annie!" Eve said. "It's right here, just like you said it would be."

"Good. Now leave it there." I didn't have to mention this to Jim and Norman. They were conscientious enough not to forget that if we tampered with the evidence, it might affect the police case later. But it never hurt to give Eve a gentle reminder. "Get out of there," I told her. "And don't forget to lock the front door behind you. I'll meet you back at Bellywasher's."

Feeling far more encouraged than I had since the day Alex first called to tell us he'd been arrested, I opened Edward's desk, careful not to disturb anything.

But what I was looking for—what Jim, Norman, and Eve had already found—wasn't there.

Discouraged and bewildered, I plunked down into Edward's desk chair. The leather was as soft as butter, so I should have felt like I was sitting on a cloud. Instead, when something stabbed my thigh, I squirmed. It reminded me of the poke I'd felt the day before when that woman on the crowded Old Town street jabbed me with her purse.

Curious, I slid my hand down between the body of the chair and the cushion. My fingers traced the outline of an envelope. It was the corner of that envelope that had dug into my leg. I pulled out the envelope, examined it, and my mouth fell open. It was a greeting card addressed to Edward. Beth's return address sticker, the one with her name printed right on it, was still stuck in the corner.

Two things occurred to me. One was that Beth had said she'd sent her blackmail letter to Edward inside a sympathy card. The other was something Tyler had told me—no one was stupid enough to keep a blackmail note, especially if that someone was planning to kill the blackmailer. But when I turned the envelope over in my hands, all was explained. At least all about why Edward had kept the card in the first place. It had never been opened. I pictured Edward bringing it into the office with the mountain of sympathy cards he must have received when Vickie died. He'd dropped this card, and it had slid down into the cushion and been forgotten.

Which meant Edward didn't know about Beth's demands. Not about how she wanted Jeremy to play soccer. Not about how she wanted Michael to get that big, fat promotion.

I tapped the card against my chin, thinking, and I should have been more confused than ever. Not so! Suddenly, everything made perfect sense. Now if I could only find what I'd come to find in the first place, I'd know I was on the right track.

Reenergized, I scanned the room, wondering where Edward might tuck something so incriminating. Michael, Scott, and Chip weren't as careful, which was why Jim, Norman, and Eve had found their copies of Sonny's newsletter so easily. Edward, I suspected, had more to lose.

After a couple minutes of thinking and a couple more of searching, I found it, finally, tucked under the desk blotter. Just as I expected, the newsletter was dog-eared and Sonny's class schedule was circled in red. The words *Saturdays only* were underscored with heavy slashes.

I tucked the newsletter and the sympathy card back where I'd found them and hurried out of the house. I had one more stop to make and once I did, I'd have everything I needed to prove who killed Vickie and Beth, and why. For now, I had one piece of the puzzle, and it was a big one. I knew that Edward wasn't the only one who knew his wife was stepping out on him. All of them—Edward, Michael, Scott, and Chip—every one of the husbands knew what his wife was up to on Tuesday nights.

* * *

OAKWOOD CEMETERY IN FALLS CHURCH, VIRGINIA, is right off the Lee Highway. It didn't take me long to get there, and I timed my arrival just right. I parked my car just as the service finished and the mourners were walking away from Beth's grave.

Beth was much loved and the crowd was sizable. I saw Glynis and Celia standing to the side and crying, but I ignored them and hoped they didn't see me. If I was right about what was going on, Beth's funeral wasn't the place for them to find it out. I sidestepped my way through the crowd of teary-eyed mourners and found Michael looking appropriately solemn in a black suit and an understated gray-and-black-striped tie.

"I am so sorry." I didn't have to pretend to be rushed and out of breath; it was a long walk from the car and over to the gravesite. "Oh, Michael! I can't believe I missed the entire service. I had to stop at Ballston Common Mall in Arlington this morning and when I came out, my car had a flat. Doesn't it just figure!" I threw my hands in the air in frustration. "My cell phone wasn't working, either. The battery was dead. And have you ever tried to find a public phone these days? It's practically impossible."

He was distracted. Who could blame him? Michael had just seen his wife's ashes interred. The emotional undercurrent of the situation was, of course, exactly what I was hoping to take advantage of.

His answer was a throwaway designed to dismiss me as quickly as possible. "There's a public phone right there at North Glebe and Seventh Street North," he said, and it wasn't until the words were out of his mouth that he realized he'd given himself away.

This was no time to gloat, so I didn't dare crack a
smile when I said, "North Glebe and Seventh Street
North. That's the pay phone that was used to call in the
anonymous tip about Vickie. You know, the one that led
the police to her body. They had a theory that the murderer made the call. It's funny that you'd know exactly
where that phone is located."

Michael's face went as gray as the stripe in his tie.
Right before a color like hot lava shot up his neck and
into his cheeks. "It isn't funny," he growled. "It isn't anything. It's just a comment. It's just a phone. And plenty
of people know it's there."

"Of course." I backed off. There was no point in doing
anything else, at least not until I talked to Tyler and told
him about everything I'd discovered that day. "It's a public phone. On a public street. I only wish there was someone over at the mall this morning who knew where it
was. Then I could have called for a ride and gotten here
on time. You know, Michael, I really am sorry about
Beth."

His jaw was so tight, I was afraid it might snap, and
besides, I'd found out all I needed to know. I turned and
walked away.

By now, the crowd had dispersed. I saw Chip take
Glynis's arm. With one sharp look over his shoulder at
me, Scott walked over to where Celia was waiting. I
didn't see Edward at all, and I figured he was already
back in his car and headed home.

With that in mind, I took a moment to stop in the
shade of a tall standing headstone to pull out my cell and
give Tyler a call. Reception was terrible; I couldn't get a
connection. Determined, I skirted a newly dug grave
gaping like a bottomless pit in the sunshine. I ducked
under the low-hanging branches of a tree and walked

another dozen yards, hoping for a better signal. When I didn't get one, I told myself there was no hurry and turned back toward my car.

Edward Monroe stood directly in my path.

I sucked in a surprised gasp.

Edward took a step closer. "You're not very good about following advice," he said, his voice even, though there was a spark of annoyance in his eyes. "I told you—"

"To mind my own business. Yeah, I remember that." My heart beat double time and I forced myself to take a few steadying breaths. Without making it look too obvious, I looked to my right and my left out of the corner of my eye, just to see who was around. Nobody was, not within yelling distance, anyway. I reminded myself there was nothing to be gained by trying to be a hero, and decided to play it cool. With that in mind, I offered Edward a quick smile. "I appreciate your advice. It's always nice to have good friends watching your back. That's what friends are for, isn't it? They care about you."

He took another step closer. His hands balled into fists at his sides.

Oh, yeah, there was a time to play it cool, all right. But there was a time to run, too. Since cool was getting me nowhere, I gathered my courage, told myself I could sprint with the best of them even though I knew it wasn't true, and spun around.

Michael was standing not five feet behind me.

Even before I looked, I knew Scott and Chip would have my other opportunities for escape blocked. Scott was on my left, Chip on my right.

I was hemmed in and alone, and my only hope was to find a weak link and take advantage of it. This was no time to beat around the bush. "You knew your wives were stepping out on you. All of you knew." I looked from one man to the others. "You can't deny it. Not when you each have Sonny's cooking class schedule in your possession. You knew there were no cooking classes on Tuesday nights."

"Edward!" Chip stepped forward, but whatever protest he was going to offer was cut short by Edward's scorching look.

Weak link noted, and it was exactly where I thought it would be. I took a step in Chip's direction. "Just like your wives, you were all best friends, and best friends stick up for each other. That's why you all agreed to the plan, though Edward . . ." I looked back his way. "I'm pretty sure you were the mastermind. It has your cold, calculated sort of stamp on it."

"Really?" He folded his arms over his chest. "How cold and calculating is that?"

"Cold and calculating enough that you all agreed to kill each other's wives."

Talk about touching a nerve! Edward's nostrils flared. Michael fumed. Scott, who I'd probably never said more than a few words to, just about blew a gasket. As I expected, Chip dissolved into a quivering mound of mush.

"I told you!" Chip blubbered. Tears streamed down his cheeks. "I told you somebody was going to find out. I told you it was a bad idea, Edward. There was no way we could plan four murders and not think we'd get caught."

"Shut up." Edward's snarl stopped him in his tracks. "She doesn't know anything. She's bluffing. There's no way she knows. It's all just a crazy theory, so keep your mouth shut."

I made it look as casual as I could when I took another step in Chip's direction, and because I was hoping to catch them all off guard, I kept right on talking.

"Poor Beth, as soon as she told Edward what was going on with Vickie on Tuesday nights, she signed her own death warrant. She was the only one who could prove you knew what Vickie was up to, Edward. That's why she had to die. But then Michael . . ." I looked his way while I stepped toward Chip. "That's what you were talking about when you said Beth wasn't supposed to die yet. Your plan called for each of you to do a favor for a best friend. You were each going to murder one wife, but not your own. That explains Edward's alibi for the night Vickie was killed. They all had to die, but my guess is you were going to drag it out over the course of a year or so. Some of the deaths would look like accidents, like Beth's was supposed to. And poor Beth, she thought she'd be safe by blackmailing Edward. Little did she know she didn't have to. Right?" I didn't wait for Edward to answer; I breezed right on. "Jeremy playing soccer and Michael, you getting a promotion you obviously hadn't earned . . . that was Edward's payment to you, wasn't it? That was your reward for killing Vickie. And you knew exactly where to find her. Edward had probably been following her. He brought you a coaster so you could easily find the place."

"Shut up!" Edward was done talking. He closed in on me and my gut reaction told me to run. When I made a move to take off in Chip's direction, Michael came up from behind and his hand went around my arm like a vise.

"Toss her in that open grave," Edward growled. "You didn't get it right with the sauna or that bus. Maybe this will work better. We'll cover her up and they won't find her until it's too late."

Michael and Scott didn't hesitate. Chip was another story. He was as pale as the ghost I would be if I didn't

do something and didn't do it fast. Michael had my right
arm in a death grip. Scott had my left. I locked my legs
and refused to move, and when they tried to drag me, I
kicked and screamed. Even all the noise I was making
wasn't enough to block out Chip's shrieks.

"We never agreed to this. Not to this." He was hys-
terical; he fell to his knees. "We never said we'd hurt
a stranger. It's going to get us in trouble, Edward, and
it wasn't part of the plan. We said we'd kill each other's
wives. We said we'd do it because they deserved it. They
were sneaking around behind our backs. They needed to
be punished. But this is too much."

We were at that wide-open grave. I toed the edge, still
struggling to keep as far away from the hole as I could,
and when Scott and Michael tightened their grips, I
knew they were going to heave-ho me down into the
hole. Once I was down there, there was no way out. I
needed a miracle, or a friend. I'd settle for either, as long
as it was fast.

I was so busy struggling and praying and looking for
a way out, it took me a second to notice when Scott loosened his hold. Michael did the same. They stepped away
from me, and when I looked at them, both of them were
staring, mouths open and eyes wide. It didn't take me
longer to figure out why.

Glynis and Celia had stepped out from behind a headstone, and the looks of stunned disbelief on their faces
told me they'd heard everything. While the wives were
still processing what they'd learned and the husbands
were wondering what it all meant and what they were
going to do about it, I made my move. There was a shovel
nearby, and I reached down and grabbed it. I swung and
I swung hard, and at that point, I didn't care who I hit.

It turned out to be Edward, who staggered, stumbled,

and fell into the hole, where he proceeded to swear a blue streak and demanded that his conspirators help him out. But with their ringleader gone, Scott and Michael lost their nerve. They took off running. Weeping, Chip crawled over to Glynis and made a grab for her hand.

She took one look at him and wound an arm through Celia's; together, the women hurried to my side. They led me over to Celia's SUV. It had one of those in-car phone systems and the reception was perfect.

Within seconds, we had the police on the phone.

Sixteen

✖

"YOU HEARD? CHIP IS SINGING LIKE A CANARY!" I was in Tyler's arms. We were dancing, of course! He'd just cut in on me and Alex, and now he twirled me. I waited until the familiar Bellywasher's scenery settled down before I even tried to answer.

"I'm not surprised," I said. "It was obvious all along that Chip was upset about something. He felt terrible about what was going on; Vickie's murder, Beth's, the idea that one of these days, Glynis was going to be next."

"Apparently, that's what he started out feeling so guilty about, knowing that his own wife was going to be murdered. But people like that are all alike. Selfish through and through. By the time it was all over, I think Chip was feeling less worried about Glynis and more concerned that he was going to get caught. It's no skin off my nose why he decided to talk." Tyler smiled. No, really, I mean it. Detective Tyler Cooper actually smiled! "Whatever gets him to squeal on his coconspirators is fine by me. They've all lawyered up, and it's not going to do them one bit of good. We're going to lock the whole bunch of them up for the rest of their days."

The thought was enough to send a cloud skittering over what had been, until that moment, the happiest day of my life. Believe me, it wasn't that I felt sorry for Chip, Scott, or Michael, and I especially didn't feel sorry for Edward. Chip had confirmed my suspicion that the plot was Edward's brainchild from the start. As soon as he found out what Vickie was doing on Tuesday nights, Edward began following her. And when he learned that the other women were doing the same thing . . . well, Edward was the kind of man whose personal power was hard to resist. He'd proved that when he convinced the other husbands that their wives needed to be punished.

"Poor Vickie and Beth," I said. "And poor Celia and Glynis. I invited them to the wedding, you know. But I'm not surprised they didn't come. They're going to need a lot of time and some serious counseling to get over everything that's happened. I can't even imagine how hard it must be for them. To think that your husband is part of an elaborate plan to kill you . . ."

"He is not. Never would." An ear-to-ear smile on his face, Jim cut into the dance, and Tyler didn't protest. Eve was standing near the bar and he went over and gave her a peck on the cheek. My happiness factor shot up another couple notches. That's what happens when a best friend sees her best friend in love. Would Eve and Tyler end up like Jim and me, with wedding rings on their fingers and the warm promise of years of happiness adding to the glow of every day? Honestly, I couldn't say. But I could hope. From the love-struck look in Tyler's eyes when he gazed at Eve, I could tell he did, too.

And who could blame him for looking at her like she had stepped out of a dream? That day, Eve was resplendent in a dress she'd bought the summer before, hung in her closet, and promptly forgot she even had. It was a satin sheath with a funky little beaded bolero, so like the one I'd lost beneath the wheels of that bus, it was uncanny. Her dress was robin egg blue, a perfect maid-of-honor complement to my sapphire gown.

Yeah, the strapless one with the rhinestone-studded bodice and the full skirt that looked like mounds of whipped cream. The one that Marie just happened to have in my size.

On the hanger, the gown was so bodacious and so not me, I couldn't stand to even think about it, but once I tried it on—

"You look incredible," Jim said. "Like a fairy-tale princess."

I felt like I'd just stepped out of a fairy tale, too, and right into my own happily-ever-after. Especially when Jim scooped me into his arms and held me close. "Just so there's no doubt about it," he said, "you need to know that your husband adores you." And he kissed me to prove it.

Our wedding guests were apparently watching. They erupted in cheers and applause.

Marc, one of our cooks, had volunteered to be the DJ for the evening. When he saw that Jim and I were dancing together, he changed the song from something with an upbeat, Big Band sort of feel to one that was nice and slow.

Jim's arm tightened around my waist. I rested my head on his shoulder. We'd been so busy greeting guests and toasting since we'd said *I do*, we'd hardly had a moment to talk to each other. This was nice, swaying back and forth, curled into each other's arms. I had never been so certain of anything: This was where I wanted to be for the rest of my life.

"And I'm not just saying I love you because of the deep-fried Mars bars." There was a smile—and just a tiny smudge of chocolate—on Jim's lips.

"It was the only Scottish food I could find that didn't gross me out," I explained. "I wanted to make something more traditional, something more truly Scottish, but—"

"What could be a better tribute to Scottish cuisine!" Jim laughed. "I remember having them in the fish-and-chips shops as a boy back in Glasgow. It was a wonderful gift, and you are a wonderful woman to have thought of it."

I had to come clean. After all, this was my husband I was talking to. "Marc and Damien did the frying." Since the smoke alarms hadn't gone off, Jim probably had already figured this out.

"And it's perfect. You'll notice that Alex and the rest of my Scots relatives have eaten more than their share."

"And the African violets?"

Jim glanced around the pub at the flowers we'd placed on every table. "They're a lovely gift for our guests." His smile settled and his expression grew serious. "Only, Annie, after everything that's happened, do you still believe? I mean, in love and marriage and how two people can be together for the rest of their lives?"

It was a strange question, especially coming from my groom on our wedding day. I stepped back enough to look up into Jim's hazel eyes. "You think—"

"I think that when you solve a couple murders and they're all tied up with wives going out to meet other men, and husbands who are angry at their wives for going out and meeting other men . . . I don't know." Inside his tux jacket, his broad shoulders twitched. "I think all that might tend to make any woman a little nervous. You know, about marriage."

"Not about my marriage!" This time, I kissed him. It was just about the best way I could think to prove my sincerity. "It's sad that those relationships ended so badly. It's tragic. But that's not going to happen. Not to you and me. This is going to last forever."

His eyes gleamed. "Aye, I was hoping you'd say that. It's what I think, too."

Across Bellywasher's, Alex raised a glass and proposed another toast, and I couldn't help but smile. "Alex doesn't seem to have suffered any long-lasting effects. I'm glad it all worked out."

"And Alex knows it worked out all because of you. Thank you!" Another kiss and I'll admit it, I could have stood right there like that forever. That's how contented and happy I was.

I might have stood right there like that forever if not for the fact that another cheer went up from the crowd. I pulled out of Jim's arms (but kept a hold of his hand) just in time to see Damien carry our wedding cake out of the kitchen, and yes, I breathed a sigh of relief. It was the same understated wedding cake I had ordered from Clara: a yellow cake, frosted with chocolate mousse and tastefully decorated with a festive, ivory-colored ganache ribbon and dozens of multicolored (but not too bright) ganache stars. There wasn't a sparkler in sight, and this made me very happy.

Even if the cake was bigger than I thought it was going to be.

I hardly had a moment to think about it. Our guests urged us to cut the cake, Marc put on an appropriately upbeat song, and, hand in hand, Jim and I approached the cake table.

"It's wonderful," he said. "Like you, Annie."

"It's perfect," I agreed.

And it all was. There was nothing in the whole wide world that could ruin that moment or that day.

Even when Doc popped out of the cake.

"LIFE IS GOOD." MY HEAD ON JIM'S SHOULDER, I stood on the walkway that led up to his house—our house—and enjoyed the moment. "Everyone was so nice. And they all seemed to have a good time."

"It was the best wedding ever. Of that, I'm certain. And now . . ." He stepped in front of me so that we were face-to-face and I don't think I was imagining it: Jim looked a little nervous. He ran his tongue over his lips. "I think there are some formalities. I'm supposed to carry you up the steps and into the house and over the threshold, yes?"

I laughed, took hold of his hand, and pulled him toward the house. "Oh, no. I need you to save your energy!" Side by side, we raced up the steps together.

"And you . . ." Jim unlocked the door and pushed it open. "You can finally get a look at your home."

Now I was feeling nervous. I took a deep breath and stepped into the living room for my first look at the work Jim had planned and Alex had carried out.

My breath caught, and I smiled, twirling all around for a better view. "It's wonderful!" I said. "No more cabbage roses! No more red walls! It's all wonderfully, beautifully beige!"

And sure, I knew it before, but this sealed the deal: From that moment forward, my happily-ever-after was official.